Rescue of
the Undead

My Life Among the Undead:

Book 10

Camara M. Bragdon

My Life among the Undead Books

By

Camara M. Bragdon

Friend of the Undead

Yard Sale of the Undead

Secrets of the Undead

Carnival of the Undead

Holiday of the Undead

Reunion of the Undead

Election of the Undead

Legacy of the Undead

Quests of the Undead

DEDICATION

This book is dedicated to everyone who has ever taken a stand against evil and injustice. Keep fighting to make the world a better place for everyone.

CHAPTERS

Prologue:
Seven Years Ago

It was a family friend, Matt Turner's birthday. My father, Timothy Anderson, had invited him and several of their mutual friends to our house for a birthday dinner. All nine of us listened as the blond haired man in the wheelchair told us about an incredible opportunity. Matt's steel-gray eyes lit up with excitement as he explained. "It'll just be a consultation at first, and then I'll have to go in for some routine medical tests to make sure I can do the treatment. Just imagine in six months, I'm going to be able to walk again."

My father, a tall, muscular police detective, raised a skeptical eyebrow at his friend. "Isn't that impossible?" he asked with doubt in his baby blue eyes.

Natalie Baker broke in. "Actually, medical and veterinary science has progressed significantly in the past few years. Just last night, Andrew and I were reading an article about it."

Her husband, Andrew, looked up from his piece of chocolate fudge cake at her in confusion in his hazel eyes. "We were?"

The plump veterinarian narrowed her brown eyes at him. "Yes, you mentioned how interesting the article was."

"It was a very fascinating article about sick little kittens," the black man said in a vain attempt to back-peddle.

"Dad, the article was about a puppy," Andrew and Natalie's seven-year-old daughter piped up.

"Ooh, exposed by your daughter, Andrew," said Chris Lopez, as he gave the girl a high-five. "Nice one, Jenny."

"Thanks, Uncle Chris," the girl replied with mischief in her ice-blue eyes,

"That's what I'm here for," the thirty-something-year-old dispatcher replied. He was a short, thin man with olive skin and dark hair.

"I thought it was because you're Uncle Dusty's boyfriend."

Chris smiled at his honorary niece as his gentle brown eyes danced. "True."

"The article," continued Natalie, clearly ignoring her

husband, "was about the use of robotics to help a dog with a spinal injury to walk again. It is possible, Timothy."

"That's awesome," Dad said, relief in his voice as he combed back his short brown hair.

"Guys, it checks out," Matt assured everyone.

"And I'm going with him," Chris said. "So, it'll be fine." He and Matt had been best friends since college, and both worked for the county as 911 dispatchers." Maybe, they'll have a cure for my spina bifida."

"That would be awesome, honey," Henry "Dusty" Williams said as he put an arm around Chris. The police detective with the dusty-blonde hair smiled at him. It was easy to see how much the men loved each other.

"Yeah," Chris replied as he glanced at the metal forearm crutches he used for balance, "I wouldn't have to use those anymore."

"Shelly," Natalie remarked to me, "are you okay? You've been pretty quiet this whole time."

"I'm fine," I said quickly. It was a lie, but no one would believe me if I told me what I was really thinking. I wanted to tell

Matt not to go because this would be the last time we would see him. I wanted to tell them about the ominous dreams I'd been having the past few nights. Dreams of him disappearing off the face of the earth. Who would believe a lowly Wal-Mart employee and her disturbing dreams? I said nothing more to the rest of the party but couldn't escape the dread hovering in the back of my mind.

It was late at night about a week later when I heard the front door open. I got out of bed and opened my bedroom door just in time to see my father and brother trudging upstairs. The hollow look on their faces told me something was terribly wrong. "Dad, what's going on?" I asked.

"Matt's missing," he said as he numbly hung up his black overcoat on a peg in the hall closet.

"What do you mean?" I asked, even though I knew the answer.

"He never returned from his medical consultation."

"What?" I was shocked and horrified that my dreams had come true. "What about Chris?"

"He has the stomach flu and ended up not going," Robin replied.

I looked at the rookie police officer and the seasoned detective and knew they weren't telling me everything. "Something else happened, didn't it?"

"Matt's apartment is completely clean out," Robin said.

"What do you mean?" I asked.

"It's completely vacant!"

Chapter One:

Mysterious Disappearances

Several figures are breaking out pieces of sparkling gold.

Sweat is running down their backs as they pull pieces of

precious gems from the wall. Clouds of black dust swirl around

them as they toss the stones into a rickety cart on a track. A

middle-age minotaur is pulling the heavy load. He stumbles on

the ground. He can barely move as blood from a recent whipping

trickles down his back.

A hideous creature composed of silver bones connected

only by muscles and ligaments kicks him in the stomach. "Get

up," the creature snarls.

"I can't," the man whimpers.

"Try." The bone creature takes a battle-axe made from

iron bones and slices the hamstrings on the bovine's legs.

The half-man, half-bull lets out an agonizing scream of pain. My father turns around and attempts to wrestle the ax away from the bone creature. "Stop it! You're hurting him!" he orders.

"He is useless to the Mannequin King," the creature snarls.

"My wife and her friend can nurse him back to health," Dad says. "Beating him won't make him work faster. He needs to rest."

A heavy-set human with a bloodied whip and a holstered pistol steps in to break up the fight. "Stop interfering, Anderson," he orders as the whip slashes against my father's face.

Dad wipes the blood from his face. "Then tell that thing to back off, Madison. Walter is injured and sick."

"Walter needs to get back to work."

"He can't if he's injured."

"Okay." Former Detective Greg Madison aims the gun at the minotaur's head. The shot echoes throughout the cave. Madison looks down at the dead Walter in disgust. "Problem solved. Baker, Williams, clean this mess up!"

Andrew and Dusty hesitate. "Are we taking him to the

Genesis Tree?" Dusty asks, a hint of hope in his voice.

"The incinerator," Madison replies. He looks at Dad. "Still trying to be the hero?" He takes out his whip and begins to beat my father mercilessly until he is unconscious. "Let this be a lesson for everyone." He tells the other laborers. "This is no place for heroics."

"Dad!" I woke up in a cold sweat, trying to remember where I was. Home, or more precisely, the fifth floor of Castle Delorean in the magical city-state of Peregrin, a chain of hidden islands. My head pounded.

"Shelly, you alright?" my husband, Eddie Van Helsing, asked. The vampire was sitting up in bed. He looked over at me with concern in his green eyes.

"I just had a bad dream. That's all." I heard a meow as a red dot danced across the wall directly across from the foot of our bed. Our little catnip dragon, Alonzo, lept at the dot. "What are you doing up at this hour?"

"Those strange noises woke Alonzo and me up and have been going non-stop." As he ran his fingers through his hair, the short jet black curls fell between them. "So, I decided to give him some exercise." He pressed the laser button on his phone. We watched as the little blue furry creature attempted to catch the red dot. Even though their bodies are serpentine, catnip dragons are really an adorable cat-dragon-hybrid and are fantastic pets. Alonzo flapped his green, butterfly wings as he tried to catch the laser.

A long, ear-splitting ping filled the bedroom. Alonzo gave a frightened meow and flew onto the end of the bed. He buried himself under the covers.

We both cupped our hands over our ears. "You've got to be kidding me!" I shouted above the noise. Alonzo wormed his way up between us and decided to sit on my chest. I was willing to sacrifice the hearing in one ear and began to scratch his head. Instantly, the little dragon began to purr as he tucked his head underneath my chin.

"At least it's not another tremor this time!" Eddie shouted.

Then I realized something. Here I was Shelly Van Helsing, the vampire queen of Peregrin with the ability to telepathically communicate with the undead shouting with my husband. *Thank god for that because Rupert and the staff would not be thrilled about cleaning the castle again*, I told Eddie.

Considering that no one in the queendom has been getting any sleep for the past fifteen nights, I don't blame him for not being thrilled.

I nodded as I stopped petting the dragon, who promptly batted at me with one of his paws. I got the message and continued to pet him.

The weird noises followed by tremors had been going on both day and night for almost a month. Fortunately, nobody had been hurt, just really annoyed and sleepless. My Minister of Science had been away visiting family, so he was no help.

Finally, the noise stopped, and we were able to hear again. "What was your dream about?" Eddie asked.

"My dad and his friends from Pembrook were miners in a chain gang. There was this minotaur who was pulling a heavy cart filled with gems. He had passed out, and this bone creature began to kick him. Dad tried to stop him, but then the creature sliced the old guy's hamstrings."

"Bone creature?" Eddie interrupted.

"Yeah, like a walking skeleton with ligaments. Anyway, there was this a-hole detective, Greg Madison, who my dad worked with. He shoots the old man in the head and tells Andrew and Dusty to take him to the incinerator."

"Andrew and Dusty?"

"Dad and Bruce's old friends from Pembrook." About seven years ago, Dad, my brother, Robin, and I had come to this fantastical world when I unknowingly opened a magical portal through time and space.

"Weird."

I nodded. "That's not all. The bone creature said that the minotaur was useless to the Mannequin King and couldn't be taken to the Genesis Tree."

"What's a Genesis Tree?"

"I don't know, but I think it could've helped the minotaur. The worst part was when Madison whipped Dad until he was unconscious and bleeding." I hadn't realized how bad the dream had affected me until Eddie slipped his arm around my shaking body.

Alonzo decided to switch places, and he jumped onto my

unsuspecting husband's chest. Eddie let out an oomph. "You think it was a bad dream or a vision?"

"I'm not sure." This was a downside to being someone with psychic abilities. When I am sleeping, I can never be sure if my dreams are just dreams or visions. "Maybe it was my subconscious telling me I should reconcile with Dad and Amelia." Eddie nodded in agreement. "Could be. You haven't spoken to them in over three months."

It had been a long time since I had spoken to my dad and my stepmom. Unfortunately, learning that your parents have lied to you about a long-lost, evil twin sister, your deceased mother, and your royal heritage can put a massive strain on your relationship with them. I'm not kidding about the evil twin part. My sister, Rachel, is evil to her very core. She had assassins try to kill me. One almost succeeded but ended up turning me into a vampire. She had ruled Peregrin with an iron fist before I helped overthrow her. "I think I need to go back to Zephyr and talk to Dad and Amelia."

"I think we can leave late Friday afternoon. You're booked all this week. You're scheduled to meet with the ambassadors from Calamaria Thursday afternoon after you see the plans and the building site for the public library. You've got a cabinet meeting the following day and the opening of the public park the day after, followed by more and more meetings with various people."

I looked at Eddie. "What? Have you switched jobs recently? You're now my private secretary, and no longer my Guardian."

"I'm letting Gunther keep his job. I just need your schedule to make sure you're safe." He leaned over and kissed me as he stroked my short brown hair.

This little move made our catnip dragon unhappy. Instead of using his wings, Alonzo climbed off Eddie and walked on top of me to get to the other side. He jumped down and darted under the bed where we wouldn't bother him.

"Thanks, honey." "I'll call Cassius tomorrow to ask him to have the Monte Carlo ready for Friday. Goodnight, Eddie." I snuggled up to him.

My husband turned off the bedside lamp and slipped his arm around me. "What's left of it."

The next morning, we walked down to my office on the first floor. The first thing I noticed was that my private secretary's desk was empty. "Gunther's usually here by now. I wonder where he is."

"He didn't call in sick. Unless he called you," Eddie replied, checking his phone to see if our employee had contacted us. Nothing.

"I'll give him ten minutes before calling him." I unlocked my office door and settled behind my large oak desk. I turned on the computer and checked my email. Even being a queen doesn't exclude you from spam email. I deleted the spam and checked the rest. Most of it was requests to meet with various dignitaries.

Eddie sat at a smaller desk to my right. He turned on his computer and checked his email to make sure that each place I was supposed to be was safe and secure. As my Guardian, he is my bodyguard and the king consort. He takes this role pretty seriously.

I heard a knock on the doorframe, and I looked up to see

Gunther Hornicus, my Private Secretary. "Good morning, Gunther," I said. I decided not to make a big deal out of his tardiness.

The satyr wiped some remaining tears from his brown eyes. He was in his fifties with two curved horns protruding from the top of his balding head. "I apologize for being late, your Majesties." His usually pressed navy dress pants over his two brown goat-shaped legs looked like he had slept in then. In fact, his whole outfit: the white dress shirt under a brown and green striped vest, was disheveled. He wasn't even wearing a tie. I had never seen him in wrinkled clothes before. He looked like a wreck, and that worried me.

"Is everything okay, Gunther?" I asked.

The half-man, half-goat began to needlessly smooth out the wrinkles on his pants. "I need to take some personal days," he said, not answering my question.

"Of course. Is everything alright?"

The satyr put his hand up to his mouth and swallowed hard before answering. "Something came up that I need to take care of right away," he replied, not meeting my eyes. I thought he would burst out crying.

"When do you need to leave?"

"Now. I've done all my work, and your schedule's all set for the week."

I wanted to ask him what was wrong, but I had a feeling that no matter how hard I pressed, Gunther wouldn't divulge anything to me. "When do you think you will be back?"

"I'll be back Friday morning," the satyr answered.

I nodded my approval, and Gunther abruptly thanked me before leaving my office. Once he had left, Eddie spoke up. "Whoa, something's really bothering him. I've never seen him wear wrinkled clothes."

"I think he was crying before he got here. Do you think someone in his family died?"

"If a family member died, why wouldn't he tell us?"

I shrugged. "Whatever it is, he has his reasons. I just really hope it works out." We both sat in silence until I remembered to call Cassius about our trip this weekend. Cassius and Gunther were good friends, and the airship captain might know something. "I'm going to give Cassius a call." I dialed the number, and the deep voice of the 600-year-old vampire captain of the *Monte Carlo* greeted me. "Good morning, Cassius, Eddie and I are going to Zephyr this weekend, and I was wondering if your airship would be available for transport."

"The *Monte Carlo* is always at your service, Your Majesty."

"It wouldn't be any trouble?" I asked.

"Of course not. We'd be happy to oblige."

"Thank you so much, Cassius. We'd leave at 6:30 Friday evening."

"That'll be fine. Is there anything else, ma'am."

I paused trying to formulate the next words. "Is Gunther all right? He came in asking for some personal days off."

It was Cassius' turn to pause. "Probably something came up he had to take care of."

"He had been crying when he came in."

A longer pause this time. Finally, the vampire said, "I'll ask him about it. I've got to go, ma'am. We'll see your Majesties at 6:30 on Friday evening."

"See you then." Once Cassius hung up, I looked over at

my husband. "That was an interesting conversation."

Eddie looked up from reading his email. "How so? We can head out to Zephyr on Friday, right?"

I nodded. "That's not what I'm talking about. When I asked about Gunther, he said it was probably something he had to take care of. But when I mentioned that Gunther had been crying, all Cassius had said he would ask him about it."

"Okay, that's a little cryptic. You think he knows what's going on?"

"Yeah, but for whatever reason, he's not telling us." I sighed. "Hopefully, everything will work out."

The rest of the week passed without incident. I met with various dignitaries, checked on the plans of the new library, and opened up the new public park. It was Thursday afternoon while I was meeting with the architect for the new library when I received a strange request and an unexpected resignation.

Colleen Tibias, the main island's best architect, according to her website, was in the conference room on the first floor of the castle with Eddie and me. She wore a navy pantsuit over her black and white bovine-shaped legs. The blueprints for the four-story library were laid out on the large oak table when my husband and I arrived to meet her. "It's great to finally meet you," I said to the minotaur as I reached out to shake her hand.

She pulled her hand away. "Forgive me, your Majesties, I'm fighting a bad cold and don't want you to get sick."

I was about to tell her vampires don't get sick, but I let it slide as I was more interested in the blueprints. There was an entire floor dedicated to the children's area, complete with three meeting rooms, one with a stage. "These plans look great."

The minotaur nodded. "Thanks. I spoke with a couple of my colleagues who have constructed various libraries." Her black and white cow's tail swished back and forth happily, and then it stopped. "May I ask you a question, your Majesty?" she asked as she nervously ran a hand through her sparkly midnight black, long hair.

"Sure," I replied. ``What is it?"

"Well, it's about my brother. He lives in Zephyr and is deaf. My husband and I talk to him every week, but I haven't heard from him for a month. He was going in for some type of experimental treatment to cure it."

My memory was triggered as I remembered the eerily similar circumstances when Matt disappeared all those years ago. "If you don't mind my asking, who suggested this treatment?" I asked her.

"His new doctor. I would've asked you about this when you first came to the throne, but I didn't want to bother you with something so trivial."

I knew I had to investigate. "You know what?" I told her. "Eddie and I are going to Zephyr this weekend. We can definitely check in on him."

Colleen breathed a huge sigh of relief. "Thank you so much. Jim and I haven't been able to see him with our work and us both being sick with the flu. His name is Walter, and he is the assistant director for the Sunny Side Up retirement home."

Fortunately, she didn't see the look of astonishment rush across my face. I managed to hide it quickly and maintained a serious expression. "No problem at all. We'll check in on him, and let you know."

She was about to shake my hand but stopped herself.

"Sorry, I don't want to infect you with my cold. Once again, thank you so much." She gathered up the blueprints and was about to leave when she asked. "Where is Mr. Hornicus?"

"He had some personal business to attend to. He'll be back tomorrow."

"Okay, I was just wondering. Can I make a suggestion, your Majesty?"

"Sure."

"I would recommend getting Mr. Hornicus, an assistant."

"That's a great idea, Shelly," Eddie said.

I nodded in agreement. "I'll put out the ad as soon as possible." I made a mental note to get started on the job advertisement as soon as I had a free moment.

We said our goodbyes. Just as the architect left the conference room, I looked at Eddie. "Did you hear what she said?" I asked.

"Yeah, Gunther really needs an assistant, especially someone to cover for him when he goes on leave, like now."

"No, not that! Colleen's brother is named Walter. Just like the minotaur in my vision."

"Okay, maybe that's just a coincidence," Eddie suggested, but even he knew full well that it wasn't. He reconsidered his last sentence. "Your visions always come true. I think we need to do an extra hour of training tonight."

I nodded. "That's exactly what I was thinking." Sometimes, Eddie and I will have a movie or board game night, but ever since we became king and queen, every Thursday night, we have weapons training. It's intense but very rewarding in many ways.

We were about to leave the conference room when the head cook walked in with a piece of paper in her hand. Mabel Grimm was a dwarf in her mid-eighties. She was the royal cook for the entire castle, but the sad expression on her face told me that something was about to change. "May I have a word with your Majesties?"

"Sure, what's up?" I asked.

The dwarf was taken aback by my statement. She was apparently still not used to my casual attitude. She blinked her grey eyes. "This is my retirement letter," she replied.

"Retiring?" I was surprised.

"Yes, I've been the royal cook for over sixty years. I think it's time for me to hang up my chef's hat and spend more time with my family." I momentarily wondered if my reign had led up to this, but Mabel quickly assured me that it wasn't. "I have been thinking about this for over a year now. I just wanted you to get settled into your position as the new queen."

"Okay, but we are going to throw you a retirement party," I said as I mentally thought about the wording of my next job advertisement.

She smiled. "I knew you would be understanding, your Majesty."

That night after dinner, Eddie and I were in the training room. I gripped the red hilt of my sword, Knowledge, with both of my hands. The sixteen-inch silver sword with the red leather hilt is a birthday gift from Eddie. It's not just any sword though. In fact, it is an enchanted sword that can turn into a book at my command. I swung it expertly at my husband who quickly deflected the sword with his golden war scythe, Vengeance. This six-foot scepter has a ring of sapphires at the top of the silver handle, but don't let that fool you. The two-foot-long curved blade on top of the sapphires makes it a deadly weapon, especially in Eddie's skilled hands. "You know what we need?" I said as I took a quick step aside to avoid the scepter's swing. "We need a danger room."

Eddie lifted up his shield to prevent a blow from Knowledge. "A what?"

"A danger room like they had in X-Men. As much fun as I like battling you in training, I wouldn't mind training where we are fighting something together."

"That'd be quite the ambitious plan, technology-wise. I don't even know anyone with that high level of technological expertise."

An ear-piercing ping erupted through the room. Eddie and I both dropped our weapons and cupped our hands over our ears as the noise went on for over ten minutes. My head was pounding. Vampires don't get headaches, but there was always an exception. I picked up my sword and said, "Without power, there is no Knowledge." Green sparks formed around the sword as it transformed back into a red leather-bound book. "I think training's over for tonight."

Eddie picked up Vengeance. "Let's call it a night and head to bed."

We headed up to our suite on the fifth floor of the castle. Alonzo greeted us by rubbing his face on our feet. "Hi, Alonzo!" I said as I bent down and petted the catnip dragon. He meowed happily and followed us into the kitchen, weaving between our legs. Eddie did the nightly dance of stepping around the catnip dragon without tripping or dropping his wet food. He gobbled down his food and then looked up at us in the hopes of getting more food. Another ear piercing ping filled the air, and Alonzo ran to our bedroom for his safe space under the bed.

The sound stopped a minute later, but the lights were bothering our eyes so we decided to eat by candlelight. Eddie heated up the leftover eggplant lasagna from the night before, and we both ate wearily.

I rubbed my temples. "This pinging has got to stop before someone loses their hearing." I finished the last bite of my food. "Do you have any ideas where it could be coming from?"

Eddie shook his head. "I've exhausted all my resources.

Isn't Dr. Wandasen supposed to be back from vacation on Monday?"

I nodded. "I've already emailed him to look into it when he gets back." I stifled a yawn. "I'm exhausted. I need to get plenty of sleep before I meet with Dad and Amelia." I got up from the table, grabbed my dirty dishes, and headed over to the kitchen sink.

"Are you ready to meet with them?" Eddie began to clear the rest of our dishes off the table.

"I don't know," I admitted as I plugged the kitchen sink with a rubber stopper and began to fill it up with water and a couple of squirts of dish soap. "I don't know what to say to them," I said as I began to hand wash a plate in the dimmed kitchen. As much as I love him, I don't trust Eddie's skills with hand washing plates. I have seen too much residue left behind. He's a much better dryer. "Am I wrong for still being angry with them?"

Eddie kissed me on the cheek. "Not really, but I really think you need to patch things up with them." He wiped a couple of dishes dry and put them away in the cupboard. "They should have told you about your sister years ago."

I sighed. "I miss talking to them. It would be nice to patch things up with them." We finished cleaning up in silence and went to bed. Sleep evaded me most of the night, and when it came, I tossed and turned as one strange image swirled about in my head: *A large triangle looms over silhouetted figures. Inside the center of the triangle is a black and red spiral moving both in and out at the same time. An eye sits on each point of the triangle.*

Chapter Two:
Mannequins Make Terrible Tour Guides

The next morning was weird. I barely got any sleep and stumbled through my busy day as if I were a zombie. For one thing, Gunther never showed up for work. Both Eddie and I tried calling him but received only his voicemail. I wrote it off, rationalizing the satyr might need some extra time off for whatever he was doing.

With our bags packed and asking a castle staff member to feed Alonzo, Eddie and I arrived at the dock on his motorcycle. The massive, magnificent airship, the *Monte Carlo*, hovered about 200-feet above ground, awaiting our arrival. The huge gray balloon is twice as long as a football field and just as high. The gondola, a huge clipper ship's hull, is tethered to the balloon with twelve strong suspension cables. Two engines similar to a jet plane are on either side of the hull. The bust of a blue lion is proudly displayed as the *Monte Carlo's* figurehead. Every time I see it, I'm always impressed.

A tall, barrel-chested vampire with a patch over his right eye was waiting on board. His hands were jammed in the pockets of his unzipped, signature black leather 1940's panzer jacket over his flight uniform: a crisp white shirt and tie and black dress pants. He lifted the brim of his red beret with the blue lion surrounded by three fleurs-de-lis to greet us. "Good evening, your Majesties!" he shouted. "Are you ready to board?"

"Yes, we are!" I shouted back.

The vampire picked up a wooden ladder and tossed it down to us.

Using his shrinking spell, Eddie had previously shrunk our luggage down to fit inside his pocket. He used the same spell and shrank his motorcycle down to the size of a Hot Wheels toy. He picked it up off the ground and slipped into his pocket. This way carrying things would be a breeze. We quickly scaled the ladder and greeted Cassius. "Thanks for taking us to Zephyr on such short notice," my husband told him.

"Not a problem at all, sire. It's my pleasure to serve your Majesties." Cassius said with a smile. He radioed in via the comlink in his ear. "Three transportation spheres to the main deck, please."

Moments later three floating orbs the size of a basketball appeared in front of us. We all grabbed a hold of each one and were suddenly teleported to the fourth deck. Cassius led us to the room Eddie and I always stayed in. Eddie removed the luggage from his pockets, laid them on our bed, and waved his hand in a circular motion. "Maximum five!" he said, invoking the magic spell. The two suitcases grew to their normal sizes.

"Your Majesties, may I ask about the nature of your trip?" Cassius asked.

"Yeah, sure," I said. "I'm going to patch things up with my father and stepmother. We had a falling out when I found I was royalty."

Cassius nodded sympathetically. "I hope everything works out well for you."

"Cassius, I know you're good friends with Gunther."

The captain nodded, but there was hesitancy in his voice

when he spoke. "He's my best friend."

"He didn't show up for work today, and we couldn't get a hold of him. Is he okay?"

A look of fear flashed across Cassius' face as he quickly blocked my mind-reading attempts. "I'm needed on the bridge," he said before quickly leaving us.

Eddie and I exchanged a puzzled look at the retreating airship captain. "Wow!" my husband exclaimed. "Did you see the look on his face? It was as if you sentenced him to death."

"I know. What was that all about?" I asked.

"Did you get a chance to read his mind?"

"No, he intentionally blocked my telepathy."

"Weird." Eddie suddenly smiled. "I have an idea. Would you like me to do some undercover work?"

"No, I don't want to spy on anyone. Political leaders spying on people usually lead to bad things." I replied as I unzipped the front pocket of the smaller suitcase. I rummaged through our array of weapons. I had insisted on bringing them because of a nagging, uneasy feeling in my gut. I found the blank legal pad and a pencil. I leaned against the headboard and began to write out my apology to my parents.

"Good point," Eddie got up. "I think I'll get in an early lesson." Cassius had started giving my husband lessons on piloting the *Monte Carlo* about two weeks ago, and Eddie loves every minute of it. "Have fun writing." He gave me a quick kiss and left me alone.

I began to write: "Dad and Amelia, I want to--" I tore out the lined paper and crumpled it before tossing it across the room, missing the wastebasket by several inches. I began to write again. "Dad, Amelia, I know you meant well to hide Mom's heritage from me, but--." Too accusing. Another paper crumbled. I shut my eyes and tried to think of the best way to tell my father and stepmother that I still loved them, even though they lied to me about my mother and my sister. It had been a long past couple of months since our huge fight, and I missed talking to them, getting advice or just hearing their voices. I began to write again and crumbled up more papers in the process. Finally, I set the almost empty legal pad aside and sighed. I debated calling Dad and Amelia but decided to wait until we saw them. My gut told me something was wrong. "I'm probably overreacting," I said to myself.

I brushed my worries aside as I decided to dial the number for the Sunny Side Up Assisted Living Center. We would arrive in Zephyr in about three hours at 9 o'clock, but according to their website, the facility was open 24/7. "Thank you for calling the Sunny Side Up Assisted Living Center: Where Every Day is a Sunny One." said a way-too cheerful recording. "Our facility is open 24 hours a day, seven days a week. If you know your party's extension, please dial it now. If you would like to inquire about residency, please press 1. If you would like to speak with someone in administration, please press 2. If you have an emergency, please press 3. For all other inquiries, please press 4. Otherwise, press zero to speak with an operator."

Since I didn't know Walter's extension, I pressed zero and listened to the same uber cheerful voice thanking me for calling and informing me that someone will be with me momentarily. No one was with me momentarily. My patience finally broke after listening to twenty-five minutes of continuous yodeling. What kind of moron thought yodeling would be great call-waiting music? I finally hung up and redialed the number. This time I pressed the emergency number and was still on hold for ten minutes when Eddie walked back into our room. "You want to hear the worst on-hold music?" I asked him.

He gave me a wary look. "I guess so?"

I pressed the speaker button and subjected my husband to more yodeling. The exaggerated look on his face made me chuckle. "You think that's bad? I've spent almost forty-five minutes listening to this."

"Why?"

I gave up and ended the phone call. "I've tried to get a hold of someone at Sunny Side Up, but nobody's answering."

"I thought it was supposed to be open 24/7."

"Apparently they didn't get that memo." I tossed the legal pad aside. I would have to wing my apology, instead of reading it. I hopped off the bed. "Okay, slight change of plans. When we get to Zephyr, we are going to Sunny Side Up Assisted Living Center first. I need to figure out what is going on."

We arrived in Zephyr about two hours later. Both Eddie and I took our weapons with us. When we teleported to the ground, my husband took out his mini motorcycle and placed it on the pavement. He waved his hand over it and said, "Maximum five!" Instantly, the motorcycle grew back to normal. We climbed aboard, and we sped off to the nursing home.

Apparently, the website for the Sunny Side Up Assisted Living Center needed more current pictures. Eddie nearly missed the driveway due to the overgrown grass that hadn't seen a lawnmower in a long time. Yellow paint was slowly peeling off the siding, and a few banged-up shutters clung to the loose screws that were holding them to the two-story Victorian. "I guess it's true you can't believe everything you see on the internet," I said once Eddie turned off the engine and put the kickstand down.

Eddie pointed to the lights coming from the windows. "At least, someone's here." We could see moving figures silhouetted in the lighted windows

"They've got some really crappy landscapers," I said as we wove our way to the front door. Music and laughter came from behind the big oak door. But the laughter wasn't normal. It was as if something was learning to laugh for the first time, but could not understand human emotions at all. I was about to knock on the door when Eddie pulled me back suddenly.

"Shelly, do you hear that?" He asked me quietly.

"Hear what? The obnoxious yodeling or the weird laughter?"

"Not that. Listen with your vampire hearing."

"Fine," I said, a little irritated. I closed my eyes and tuned into my vampire auditory sense. Normally, I could pick up the slightest heartbeats in the area, such as a vampire, but I heard absolutely nothing. I instinctively put my hand on Knowledge's hilt. "I can't hear a single heartbeat in there. Who or what is behind that door?" I asked.

"I guarantee it's nothing good." My husband looked at me as he grabbed Vengeance from off his utility belt. "Shall we find out?"

I nodded. I stepped on the threshold and rapped on the door. I don't know what I was expecting. Maybe the music and laughter suddenly coming to a complete stop as the occupants realized the king and queen of Peregrin had come to stop their evil plan. I certainly wasn't expecting them to completely ignore me. I tried knocking again, even louder this time and saying,

"Avon calling!"

No response.

"Must be a good party," Eddie remarked.

"Okay, let's see if we can get their attention another way." I stepped off the stoop, and we walked to the nearest window. I tried to peer in, but my view was blocked by a curtain.

"I could try turning into mist to see if I could get through a crack," Eddie suggested. I nodded my agreement. The vampire materialized into a green mist. He propelled his fog-like form into the air as he began to hunt for a way in.

I tried tapping on the glass, but no response. I had a great idea to get the occupants' attention, old-school style. I scooped some pebbles in the grass and tossed them against the window. One of the figures stopped whatever it was doing and stiffly walked to the window. I stepped closer as the curtain was pulled back. "Hi, my name is--AHHHH!" My friendly greeting was cut short as I came face to face with a life-like mannequin with a creepy, unnatural smile staring back at me.

It reminded me of the time my brother, my dad, and I went to the Plymouth Wax Museum to "make history come to life" as

Dad put it. I clearly could've gotten a better history lesson if I didn't mistake one of the figures for Dad when I touched its arm. Robin said he has never heard me scream so loud in his life.

I could see the wax figure's lips moving as it beckoned others to the window. The music turned off. Soon the window was filled with creepy mannequins staring at me.

Eddie, get back here now! I shouted telepathically. *We've got a big problem!*

A green mist quickly formed on the ground as my husband rematerialized next to me. "Shelly? Is everything all--Holy crap! What are those things?" He pointed to the wax figures in the window.

The window suddenly opened and mannequin hands grabbed us. With surprising strength, the things yanked us inside. They immediately let go of us and stood still. I pulled my sword from my hilt as Eddie stood by my side. *At least, we found a way inside*, I telepathically told him.

This was the only way inside really. The entire house is sealed off from the outside. Eddie told me as he looked over his shoulder at another mannequin closing the window and breaking the latch. *We were trapped and sealed off from the outside. We've got this. It isn't our first rodeo.*

True, but it's certainly the first time we've been trapped in a nursing home surrounded by living mannequins.

Fair point. I'm just waiting for one of your crazy plans to miraculously save our butts.

I thought for a moment. *I have an idea. Just play along.* "Hi, my name is Shelly, and this is Eddie." I waved my sword-free hand and nudged my husband to do the same. "We didn't mean to interrupt your party?" I hesitated on the last word as I looked around trying to decide if I had said the right thing. Dust and cobwebs had gathered on the shelves, but there were well-worn patterns in the carpet. These mannequins had moved in the exact same directions for what looked like a long time. "Did you know how loud your music was? We could hear it from the street. Isn't that right, Eddie?"

He nodded. "Super loud music."

"Does the music keep the residents awake? Because if I heard incessant yodeling all through the night, it would drive me insane. Speaking of which, I'm surprised that we have seen any of the residents here. Anyway, my father's getting on in years, and we can't take care of him. So we're looking for a long-term care facility. This place came highly recommended."

The mannequins didn't say anything which was disturbing. By the ever-changing facial expressions, I could tell they definitely understood what I was saying and weren't buying my act.

I took a step forward. "Do you mind if we take a look around just to see the facility? Then we'll leave you to your yodeling. Dad would love it here. He loves to yodel all the time. He was in a singing group called the Yodeling Boys in Blue."

They nodded and beckoned us to follow them. "Oh look, Eddie. The mannequins are giving us a tour. Isn't that nice of them?"

"Sure is."

I glanced over my shoulder as the other mannequins gathered behind me and Eddie. Oh, goody, they were going to follow us to make sure we didn't try to make a break for the door. I kept my concern hidden and put on a joyous expression.

We followed the mannequins around the building as they

gave us an unconventional tour. Each door they led us to was closed. They quickly opened a crack and pointed vaguely inside before quickly slamming it shut. By the time we got to the stairs leading to the second floor, we had seen the doors labeled kitchen, library, lounge, and dining area.

Eddie and I made approving noises so we wouldn't give away our true intentions. A rank smell filled the air as we followed our silent tour guides up the stairs. *Is that smell what I think it is?* I mentally asked Eddie.

Eddie nodded. *Decomposing flesh.*

The smell worsened as we neared the top of the stairs. The lead mannequin waved its arm in a grandiose gesture and started to head back downstairs. Even though these mannequins were made of wax and plastic, they clearly didn't want anyone finding out what was really in the residents' rooms.

"Can we take a look at the rooms?" I asked, feigning enthusiasm. "I would really like to see where my dad might be staying." I reached for the doorknob and tried to turn it. Locked. Not going to be a problem. Using my vampiric strength, I yanked the door open. A little too hard. "We'll pay for that," I told the head wax mannequin as I gently set the door aside.

"We'll just take a quick peek," Eddie said as both of us sidestepped the creature and into the room.

I've seen some awful things in my life, and this was one of the worst. A decomposing body lay in a bed. Dried blood had crusted on the pillow from what looked like a head wound. I had no idea how long the person had been dead, but I could tell she had been a resident. She was most likely killed by these creatures. Or someone had this person killed, but to what end? Eddie and I exchanged concerned, nervous looks. *Why would anyone do this?* I mentally asked Eddie.

I don't know, but we need to get out of here, Eddie replied. He whirled around as he swiftly took Vengeance out. The lead wax figure charged at us but fell with one quick swipe from the war scythe's blade. Black, bubbling blood spewed out, and I stepped out of the way, expecting it to be acidic. When it hit the bedcovers, it did nothing out of the ordinary.

I pulled Knowledge out of the sheath and quickly dispatched another wax figure as my husband and I pressed our backs against each other to battle the creatures. "We seem to do this type of thing a lot.”

"Yeah, we're getting pretty good at this," Eddie took out three of the creatures with another deadly swipe. Sirens wailed in the distance, getting closer and closer. "Someone here must have called the police!"

A wax figure rushed me. I split it in half with a powerful swing from my sword. "Good. They need to know about this."

A large black portal opened up in front of us. A man I had only met once during my father's time in law enforcement. James Mallory, chief of the Pembrook Police department, was heavier than I remember. He wore an expensive navy suit with A red silk tie. His black toupee waved in the portal's wind. He still looked like a weasel.

Standing next to him was a tall, thin man in an expensive black suit with a black dress shirt and a blood-red tie. He had long, green hair cascading past his shoulders. He looked like Fabio on steroids.

For only an instant, the air around him wobbled, and Eddie and I saw who he really was: a creature I had never seen before in my entire life. His red skin sheened like wet blood.

Bright orange flames encircled his black skull-like head. His green hair was actually thousands of snakes weaving all around his head. He snapped his fingers and vanished in a puff of inky smoke

A second black portal opened, and I immediately noticed something different about it. An open wormhole creates a powerful wind which will pull everything into its path. This wind only pulled in the wax figures into the portal, never touching Eddie and me. Soon we were the only people left standing in the building.

The police sirens got louder and closer, and my husband and I could hear heavy footfall outside the building. A loud crash echoed through the empty retirement home as a large battering ram took the front door off its hinges. Police officers in heavy riot gear burst in with their weapons drawn. "Zephyr Police! Drop your weapons!" One of the officers shouted at us.

Eddie and I did as we were told. The sword and the war scythe clattered to the hardwood floor. I immediately put my hands up and spread my fingers as wide as they would. My husband followed my lead.

"On the ground now!" an elfin officer shouted. His hands shook as he held his gun. Great! Just what we needed. An untrained rookie officer.

We slowly got down on our knees with our hands still up. Several more officers rushed in and surrounded us. I glanced at Eddie. "We've got a lawyer on retainer, right?"

Chapter Three:
Colleen's Pants are on Fire

I leaned forward on the bench and rested my chin on my hands with my elbows on my knees. "This is new," I observed as I took in the room Eddie and I were currently occupying. Someone had decided to paint the room a cherry beige color. The bars were made out of reinforced steel, coupled with a force field.

Eddie nodded. "I'm surprised this hasn't happened sooner." He sat on the opposite end of the bench, one leg dangled off of the edge.

I held up my ink-smudged fingers. "We got fingerprinted. That's new and exciting."

"Yeah, because a criminal record is just what we need," he replied. "Do you really think invoking sovereign immunity is going to work?"

"That and the phone call to Judge Ruhn."

We heard the jingle of keys, and an overweight officer walked to our cell. "All right, your lawyer called," he said as he entered the keycode to disarm the force field. The electric buzz came to a sudden halt.

"We're free to go?" I asked.

The police officer gave a disgruntled nod. "Wish I had some hoity-toity lawyer to let me go free." He glowered at us as he unlocked our cell door. "Because of your 'sovereign' immunity, all charges have been dropped. Collect your belongings with the desk sergeant."

"There's no need, officer," a tall, muscular police detective in a tan suit with a white shirt and navy tie leaned against the exit as he spun a pencil between the fingers of his right hand. His dark brown hair was cut short. His blue eyes stared us down with a hint of anger and curiosity.

"Yes, Detective Anderson," the officer replied.

"Robin!" I said, "Fancy meeting you here!"

My brother shook his head as he led me and Eddie out of the holding area and into an interrogation room. Our belongings sat on a metal table. He watched us in silence as the vampire and I put on our weapon belts. Finally, he spoke with a bitter hint in his tone. "Come back for a visit?"

"Not exactly. I'm going to talk to Dad and Amelia. We had an argument." I slipped my shield bracelet back on my left hand.

"About our sister, Rachel?" my older brother guessed.

"Oh, you know?"

"Dad told me. Why didn't you tell me? I'm your brother, for Pete's sake!"

I took a deep breath as I realized who else I should have apologized to, and I felt like a real jerk. "Robin, I'm sorry," I said. "I should have told you about our sister. It all happened so fast, and I was so angry with Dad for not telling me. I wasn't thinking about your feelings. Can you forgive me?"

My brother paused for a long moment. "Of course, you're my sister. Tell me about Rachel. What's she like?"

"She's psychotic. Tried to have Shelly killed on several occasions," Eddie answered as he clipped Vengeance back on his utility belt.

Robin's eyes widened in surprise. "Really?"

I nodded. "The vampire who turned me? Her doing."

"Holy crap! Did Dad know?"

"I told him during our fight," I replied.

"I had no idea, and now I can see why you're not on speaking terms with Dad. But do you mind telling me why you guys were at Sunny Side Up Assisted Living Center?"

"One of my people asked me to check on her brother, the director of the facility. She hasn't heard from him in a while and was very concerned."

Robin raised an eyebrow at me as he crossed his arms over his chest. "One of your people?"

"Yes, I am the queen of Peregrin," I said.

"Okay," my brother answered in a tone reserved for speaking with delusional people.

"Mom was the ruler of a chain of islands several hours away from here. Eddie and I are the rulers now. I've got my own castle, private secretary, and everything."

Eddie saw Robin looking at him for confirmation."Yep, it's true. You can address your sister as 'Queen Shelly' or 'Her Majesty.'"

Robin shook his head. "This is a lot to take in, and I will be asking a lot of questions later. What exactly did you see in the assisted living center?"

"Creepy living mannequins and a dead body which I suspect belonged to one of the residents," I answered.

Robin swore. "They lied to me. Come with me to my office. I need to show you something." He led us through a long corridor and into a small private office equipped with just a desk and three chairs. A lone silver file cabinet sat on the right side of the desk. The police detective reached into his pocket and pulled out a set of keys. He quickly found the correct key and unlocked the bottom drawer. Inside was a large group of hidden files that he pulled to the front. He grabbed a thick Malina folder and shut the drawer. "What's the name of your friend's brother?"

"Walter Tibias," Eddie replied.

Robin opened the file and handed us the top page. It was a possible missing person's report on a minotaur named Walter Tibias. "Is that him?"

I pulled out my phone and searched for the text message Colleen had sent me with her brother's picture. Once I found it, I compared it with the report picture. "That's him. Who reported him missing?"

"A postal worker noticed that no one was picking up their packages. Officers were sent there and told me the whole place was cleaned out."

"That's impossible!" I said. "When Eddie and I were there, the building was fully furnished."

"I know, but when I got assigned to the case, I went to check it out myself, and guess what?"

"Fully furnished," Eddie said.

Robin nodded.

"What about the residents?" I asked.

"That's the weird thing. A few days later, they were all relocated to various facilities, unharmed, in good health, and with absolutely no memory of Walter at all. When I confronted the officers about their lie, they didn't even remember being assigned to the case. The next day, I was told they had been fired."

"If Walter was the target, wouldn't whoever did this want to get rid of potential witnesses?" I asked.

"It doesn't make sense," Eddie said.

"Walter had a disability, right?" Robin asked as he started pulling out various pages from the thick folder.

"Colleen said he was deaf."

"Was he seeing a new doctor about an experimental treatment to restore his hearing?"

I nodded.

"That got me thinking. Do you remember what happened with Matt?"

"How could I forget?" I replied. "He vanished without a trace after going in for an experimental treatment to cure his paraplegia."

"His grandparents vanished along with everything in their house, and reappeared a few days unharmed and had no memory of Matt at all."

"Of his disappearance? Eddie asked.

"It was like he never existed to them," Robin replied.

"Someone or something is wiping the memories of potential witnesses," Eddie said.

"These reports are all similar. Someone with a disability

goes in for a new medical treatment and vanishes without a trace and potential witnesses have their memories wiped."

I frowned as I furrowed my brow in thought. Something wasn't right. Then it hit me. "Why didn't Colleen call the station instead of coming to me and Eddie? She said she talked with him every week."

"That's weird because Walter had no known emergency contacts," Robin answered.

"Are you sure?"

"Positive. Walter Tibias had no next of kin. Both parents are dead and an only child. No living relatives at all."

I took a closer look at both pictures of the minotaur. They looked exactly the same, but mine looked photoshopped. "Robin, where did you get this picture?"

My brother studied the pictures more closely. "His identification card, which is clearly the same as the one you have. Why would his sister have a copy of his ID card as a picture."

"Because," Eddie said, "he doesn't have a sister. Robin, could you do a search for us? Look for a Colleen Tibias, a minotaur architect."

Robin opened up an international database and began searching. The answer he received a few moments later confirmed both my husband and my suspicions. Colleen Tibias didn't exist.

Eddie took out his phone and began to dial the head of security, Archer Wolfsguard. Once the werewolf picked up, the vampire put the call on speakerphone. "Archer, this is the king. I'm sorry to bother you at home."

"Good evening, your Majesty," the voice at the end. "Is everything all right?"

"I have you on speakerphone with the queen and her brother. I need you to check the security cameras on Thursday afternoon between the hours of 2-4."

"Sure, give me a few minutes to log into the security cameras remotely." A few minutes of silence passed, and then the werewolf spoke. "What am I looking for, sire?"

"A Minotaur came into her Majesty's office," Eddie explained. He described Colleen's appearance. "I think she may be an imposter."

"Uh, sire? I don't see anyone fitting that description near there. The only person who came to your office was Mabel."

"Check the main entrance."

"I'm sorry, your Majesty, but she isn't showing up on any of the cameras. I'll check the rest of the cameras, and let you know if she shows up."

"Thanks, Archer." Eddie hung up and looked at me. "This is a major security breach."

"Minotaurs don't disappear and reappear," I said. "They have no magical abilities."

"Whoever she is, she did lead you two to inquire about Walter," Robin pointed out.

"You're right, Robin, but I'm more concerned why she didn't show up on our security cameras," Eddie said.

"I was going to ask Dad for some advice because I think someone on the force is trying to cover up these crimes."

"What did he say?" I asked.

"I haven't talked to him since he went on sabbatical with Amelia after closing down the restaurant."

I was taken aback in shock. "The restaurant is closed?"

"You didn't know? The health department shut it down a month ago for several health code violations."

"Timothy never failed a health inspection before," Eddie said. "What happened?"

"Don't know," Robin replied. "Dad never told me the details before he went on sabbatical."

I held up my hands. "Whoa! Since when does Dad go on sabbaticals?"

"About a month ago. He and Amelia went on a two-month-long, technology-free sabbatical with Bruce and Libby." Robin pulled out his personal cell phone and played a voicemail from our father. "Robin, this is Dad," said a robotic voice that sounded like my father. 'I had to shut down the restaurant due to health code violations, but don't worry. Your stepmother and I are going on a sabbatical with Bruce and Libby to re-evaluate our lives. Good-bye."

"Robin," I said, "that isn't Dad."

"Are you sure?" my brother asked. "I'd recognize his voice anywhere."

"Dad has never used the word 'sabbatical' in his life, much

less taken one." I hesitated as I debated telling my brother about my psychic abilities. Strangers knew I was a seer but not my own family. I decided to take the risk. "Robin, I had a really bad vision of Dad. He's in trouble."

Robin shot a skeptical look at me. "A vision? What are you? A psychic and a queen?" He gave a derisive laugh. I wanted to tell him a deep, dark secret about a terrible dream I had many, many years ago, but even my husband didn't know about that dream. I forced the memory back into the recesses of my mind. "Look, you may not believe me, but I really think Dad is in trouble."

"Really, Shelly?"

I gave an exasperated sigh. "Robin, let's swing by the restaurant and Dad's to make sure everything's all right."

My brother shrugged. "All right. Eddie, your motorcycle is locked in the police garage."

Chapter Four:
My Parents Go Awol

Eddie and I followed Robin down the winding familiar road. As I wrapped my arms around my husband's waist, I could barely hear the roar of the motorcycle as I thought about what had transpired in the past few hours. What was going on? Who was kidnapping all these people and for what nefarious purposes? Deep down, I also knew Dad was somehow involved and in trouble.

Robin landed his black and green dragon, Cornelius, in front of our parents' house. Eddie parked the motorcycle and shut off the engine as we looked at the building.The two-story, red, ranch looked eerily quiet with its darkened windows. We put away our helmets in the black saddlebags and got off.

"Something's not right, Eddie," I said as I placed my hand on Knowledge's hilt.

"Yeah, I'm getting a bad vibe, too, Shelly." The vampire removed Vengeance from his utility belt and pressed the button, extending the war scythe to its deadly, six-foot length. "Be ready for anything."

I nodded in agreement.

My brother turned around and looked at us in alarm. "Are you guys expecting something bad to happen?" He asked.

"Never hurts to be prepared," I said.

"Wow, being queen has changed you!" Robin must have decided we had a good plan and drew his service revolver from his belt holster. A large pile of mail was blocking the front door of the two-story ranch.

I began to sort through the mail. The earliest piece dated back two months ago. My fears were realized. My father would have stopped the mail if he and my stepmother were going to be away for a long period of time. "We need to get inside now!" I ordered. I tried the door, but it was locked,

"Shelly, I'm not breaking down the door," Robin said.

My husband looked at Robin and then at me. Even without reading his mind, I knew exactly what he was thinking.

"I've got this." Eddie's body turned into a green mist and slid swiftly under the door. The tumblers on the doorknob turned, and the vampire let us in.

I automatically flicked the light switch by the door, but nothing happened. Lights from outside cast eerie shadows on the empty hallway walls. Where were all the pictures on the wall? Where was the wicker table Dad and Amelia used for storing their keys, mail, and other stuff people like to pile on surfaces? "Where is everything?" I asked.

"What do you—?" Robin stopped mid-sentence as he shone his flashlight around the hallway. It was completely empty. No furniture. No pictures hanging on the walls. It was as if our parents had moved.

A huge knot formed in my stomach. Something was terribly wrong. I stood perfectly still and closed my eyes so I could fully utilize my vampire senses. At least, there were no dead bodies. That was a good sign. The only heartbeats I could sense belonged to Eddie, Robin, and mine. "No one's here," I said quietly. "Eddie, can you sense anything?"

The vampire shook his head.

"We should still check it out," Robin said. "Let's split up and search room by room. I'll take the upstairs."

Eddie opened up his utility belt and retrieved two headlamps from a pocket. He tossed one to me before putting his on his head. "There has got to be a better flashlight for combat use."

"We should have Dr. Wandasen rig something up when we get home," I said. I glanced nervously at the cellar door. Eddie knew I didn't like dark basements. Bad things always happened there. "I've got the basement."

"I'll take the first floor," I said.

Robin started up the stairs when Eddie told him to stop. "What?"

Eddie dug through his utility belt and produced three earpieces. "Com links," he said as he handed them out to us. "We should be in constant contact with each other. Set the channel to four."

"Are we in contact with the *Monte Carlo* as well?" I asked. With the light from my headlamp, I turned the earpiece's dial to the desired channel before placing it in my ear. Eddie and Robin did the same.

"Not on this channel. Cassius told me this is the channel for com-link to com-link communication. Just press the earpiece to talk."

We all nodded and the men left to their respective searches, leaving me alone in the empty hallway. I slowly drew Knowledge from her sheath after I activated my shield, Truth. Then I began to search the dark floor. The first room was the living room. It was in the exact same condition as the hallway, devoid of furniture and wall hangings. I pressed the earpiece with my shield hand. "Living room is clear, guys," I said. "Literally."

"Is it completely empty?" Robin asked.

"Yeah,"

"Same with the master bedroom."

Eddie checked in. "The laundry room is completely empty, even the washer and dryer are gone."

"I'm moving on," Robin said.

"Me too."

"Same," I said. I checked the downstairs bathroom which was completely emptied of my family's belongings. I let the guys know it was clear before moving onto the kitchen and dining room. Same. Even the fridge and stove were missing. Whoever did this had literally taken everything except for the kitchen sink. I was about to report when a faint decaying drifted past my nose. To my horror, I realized we had forgotten about the stables. I ran out of the empty kitchen and out the front door. My heart pounded with dread. *Don't let it be Dad and Amelia!* I silently prayed.

Once I reached the stables, I kicked open the locked doors and gasped in horror. Two huge avian skeletons lay on the stable floor. Dried bird blood and feathers were strewn across the walls and floor. What kind of a monster would slaughter Dad and Amelia's two innocent giant eagles, Tradewinds and Scotia? If someone had done this to my beloved catnip dragon, Alonzo—I couldn't complete the thought. Tears filled my eyes.

"Shelly?" My husband's anxious voice echoed through my earpiece. "Where are you?"

I was rendered speechless as I surveyed the carnage. My eyes wandered to the back wall. A large diamond with a spiral on the inside was drawn with the birds' blood. A dripping eyeball was at each point. The scene in front of me and the uncertainty of Dad and Amelia's fates washed over me and drove me to my knees. I threw my hand over my mouth to prevent the vomit from rising from my stomach.

"Shelly, are you—?" Robin stopped mid-sentence as he and Eddie gazed at the carnage. "Oh. My. God."

"Dad and Amelia aren't here," I said softly. I felt my husband's arms around me as he gently pulled me to my feet. "I need to get out of here."

Eddie took me outside of the stable and watched in silence as I leaned against the outside wall and took in shallow, rapid breaths. "Slow, deep breaths," he gently advised as he put his hands on my shoulders.

I ignored him. "We don't know where Dad and Amelia are or what happened to them! "What if we don't find them? I couldn't bear the thought of losing both Dad and Amelia!" I could feel my heart pounding as I clenched my shaking hands. Since I had that vision, I've had this horrible feeling in my stomach that something terrible happened. That—." I struggled for the words. "Scene in there confirmed my feelings." The image brought a wave of nausea. I sank to the ground as I vomited for a few minutes before pulling myself together.

"I just want them to be okay," I whispered.

Eddie helped me up and put his arms around me. "Me too," he said softly.

"I'm sorry about this," I apologized.

"There's nothing you need to apologize for."

I managed a nod and pulled myself together. "I think we should check out the diner and then Bruce and Libby's."

The last time I went to Anderson's, it was a busy family restaurant. Not anymore. Every single window was boarded up. Even the double glass doors of the dinner's entrance had huge thick slabs of plywood nailed over them in a surprisingly great attempt to prevent breaking and entering. The yellowed health code violation clung to the wood with the help of one thick nail. We went to the employee entrance in the back. Same precautions as the front.

"What the heck?" I said as I spotted something on the pavement. Four-inch deep marks were leading away from the doors. "Are these drag marks?"

Eddie and Robin crouched beside me. My husband traced one of them with his finger. "I don't know, but something cut through the pavement."

Robin ran his fingers across a series of blackened bubbles. "I think something highly toxic caused this."

"What is going on?" I asked.

"Let's get this door opened." Robin kicked at the door and was knocked back a few feet. The door remained intact.

Eddie decided to give it a try. He held out one of his hands and said, "Nebulae!" A ball of white-hot fire rushed from his open palm and slammed into the door at an incredible speed. Nothing happened, except for the fireball ricocheting back us.

"Duck!" I ordered as we all hit the ground right as the fiery spell flew past us and into a small bush.

Eddie quickly got to his feet. "I'm going to put out that fire." He ran over and conjured up a force field to cover the flaming bush.

"There is obviously some sort of magical ward on the building, but I think I might have a collapsible crowbar to pry one of the windows open," Robin replied. He jogged back to his dragon.

I was about to say it wouldn't work because it's magic. My brother and my husband could be such idiots sometimes. I looked around and saw a bird perching on the edge of the roof. A brilliant idea came to me. I found a small rock and threw it on the roof. The stone shattered one of the skylights. The ward only protected half of the building. Like a spider, I clambered up the side of the diner with ease. Within seconds, I was walking on the flat concrete roof. I peered into the darkness through the shattered skylight and staggered back by the stench, thankfully not bodies but of rotten food.

"Shelly, where are you?" Eddie yelled.

I walked to the edge and peered down at Eddie and Robin. "I'm up here!" I shouted back. "The ward doesn't cover the roof. I found a way for us to get in."

"Hang on. I'm coming up," Eddie said as he clambered up the building.

My brother used his chlorokinesis and summoned a tree to aid him. One of the branches grew towards him. He climbed on it and soon joined us on the roof. He held his hand in front of his nose. "What is that smell?"

"Rotten food."

"Gross." He looked through the skylight at the darkened interior of the restaurant. "Do you guys smell anything else? Like bodies?"

"What are we, bloodhounds?" I asked.

"Well, you guys do have an acute sense of smell?"

Eddie set Vengeance down and began to rummage through his utility belt. He found the military-grade glow sticks, bent them and dropped through the skylight. We all watched the glow-sticks descend into the darkness and land with a soft THUD.

My eyes adjusted to the darkness, and I could barely make out the outlines of several bodies. My mind went into a panicked, hysterical mode for a moment as I thought the bodies were of Dad and Amelia. Then I realized something was off. I couldn't smell any signs of decay. What in the world was down there? "Guys, there's something down there."

Eddie leaned forward to get a better look. "I can make out

some bodies, but I can't smell any decomposition."

"We need to get a closer look," Robin said. He looked at my husband. "You got rappelling equipment in that utility belt of yours?"

"I've got something even better." Eddie popped open one of the pouches and pulled out two small guns the size of an action figure. The former wizard waved his other hand over the tiny object as he said "Maximum five." The guns grew to normal size, and my brother could plainly see what kind of gun it really was. "Grappling guns."

Robin looked at Eddie and then at me. "Are you sure you didn't marry Batman, Shelly?"

"Only if he has Batarangs on him," I said with a smile,

"Who says I didn't bring any from the armory?"

"You guys have an armory?" Robin asked.

"In my castle," I said.

"Okay, I've got to see your castle sometime!"

"You should," I said. "Eddie, I think the grappling guns won't really help us down, but it will help us when we are leaving. We can just jump."

"You two can jump," Robin said. "I, on the other hand, am not an immortal vampire and will probably break something on impact. I will summon that tree branch to lower me down."

"Okay," I said. Eddie and I shared an are-you-ready look and then a quick nod. "See you at the bottom." With that, my husband and I jumped through the darkened skylight. I landed in a graceful crouch and nearly gagged as the pungent smell of rotten food hit my heightened olfactory senses. Breathe through your mouth, I chanted silently to myself.

Robin followed us, riding on the branch like the king of the trees. I saw him dabbing fresh peppermint oil under his nose. "Could I have some?" I asked.

"Sure." He closed the bottle and handed it to me. He watched me spread it liberally under my nose. "Wow! I forgot how sensitive a vampire's heightened sense of smell is!"

"You have no idea," I said as I handed the bottle to Eddie who used about as much peppermint oil as I did.

"I'm going to see if I can turn on the lights," Robin said as he turned on his flashlight and headed in the direction of the kitchen, leaving Eddie and me to investigate the diner.

My irises quickly began to change into cat-like slits as my vampire night vision took over. It's like looking through a pair of night vision binoculars. Ten mangled bodies were spread in various pieces across the room.

I heard a crash and my husband cursing loudly. He had walked into an overturned table. He turned on a flashlight and shone around the diner. The shadows of overturned tables and chairs flickered across the walls.

When I touched one of the bodies to turn it over, I was shocked by what I felt. The body was soft and boneless. "What the frig?" I said aloud. I touched the arm only to discover plastic. I turned the body over to find a plastic, expressionless face staring back at me. I stumbled back in confusion as my mind slowly registered what I was staring at. I quickly turned over another body and was greeted by the same face. By the time I was done inspecting the bodies, I realized the horrible, weird truth. I had seen similar things at Sunny Side Up. "They're all mannequins."

"You find anything, Shell?" Eddie called from across the diner.

"Mannequins!"

"Say what?"

"Mannequins. The bodies are all mannequins!"

Eddie came over to see what I was talking about. He touched one of the torsos where the stuffing was falling out. He realized the same thing I did. The mannequins were connected to Dad and Amelia's disappearances. "What is going on here?"

I saw Robin's flashlight bobbing up and down in the dark as he came towards us. "I couldn't turn the power on, guys, but I did remember something that might help us figure out what happened here. The last time I saw Dad, he showed me his new high-tech security system. He had installed a 24/7 camera feed for 'security-purposes' and wanted to get my opinion on it. This one will keep data forever in an online database. I didn't think of it until now."

Hope sprang up in me. "Is there any way to access it?" I asked.

"I don't have that information, but Dirk might."

My brother waved his flashlight around as he talked, and I noticed the beam momentarily landed on something on the floor a few feet away from us. Without asking, I took the flashlight and searched until I found what I was looking for. A curve of a dark circle had been burned into the floor. I began to push aside upturned tables and chairs and mannequin bodies

"Shelly, what are you doing?"

I concentrated as I followed the circle which soon turned into a diagonal line. After a few minutes of clearing out a large section, I took a step back and swore under my breath before showing the men what I had discovered. The diamond was about five-feet high and four-feet wide. An eye with about three inches in diameter on each point of the diamond stared back at us. A large, motionless black spiral seemed to spin over and over in the middle of the diamond.

Eddie and Robin cursed at the same time as we all looked at the exact same symbol that was in the stables at my parents' place. "Does anyone recognize this?" Robin asked.

Eddie and I shook our heads. I pushed back the awful memory of the violent stable scene as I took a picture with my phone. "Do you think Dad's new security cameras were able to film whatever happened here?"

"I hope so," Robin said.

"What do you think happened here?"

"Don't know," Robin said hesitantly. A look of worry and concern came across his face. "I don't want to say it, but--"

I looked at my brother. "You think Dad's somehow involved with this whole mess, don't you?"

He nodded. "Yeah, he or Amelia are connected to this somehow."

"What about that symbol?" Eddie asked.

"That's new," Robin said. "This is the first time I've seen it."

I put away my worries in the back of my mind and tried to think of the reason for the symbol. A chilling thought came to me. "Guys, what if it's a warning?"

"What do you mean?" Eddie asked.

"I think Dad got caught in the crossfire, and that symbol is a warning to anyone who tries to intervene."

"What connection would he have to these disappearances?" Robin asked.

Eddie crossed his arms over his chest as he leaned

against one of the few upright tables. "I bet he started investigating."

"Yeah," Robin agreed. "Once a cop, always a cop. Somehow he got caught in the crossfire."

I remembered the heavy-set police detective who had pistol-whipped my father in my vision. "Do you remember Detective Madison?"

Robin nodded. "Yeah, he hated Dad and his friends. Why did you bring up his name?"

"He's involved as well as Chief Mallory."

"What do you mean, Shelly?"

I hesitated. I still didn't know how much my brother believed in my visions, but I had no physical evidence to prove my theory. I decided to tell him. "When Eddie and I were at the retirement center, we saw Mallory and something else clear out the building."

"Something else?" Robin asked.

I nodded as I described the man controlling the portal. "Mallory was right there with him."

"You sure?" Robin asked.

I nodded. "It's been a while, but I'd recognize Mallory's face anywhere."

"Not many people know about the portal between our worlds," Robin said.

"Whoever opened this new portal obviously does and is making friends with Dad's former evil colleagues." I paused. "That can't be a good sign."

"I think our next step should be checking in on Bruce and Libby to see if they know anything," Robin suggested.

"And if they are missing like our parents?" I asked.

"Then we have Dirk look on the security feed to figure out what actually happened here," Eddie said.

Using the grappling gun, we all rappelled out of the diner the same way we had come in. Then we went to Bruce and Libby Miller's. We encountered the same situation there as we did as Dad and Amelia's. Missing friends, completely empty house, and the same strange symbol. This time the sinister diamond was etched in black on their kitchen floor.

Robin called my brother-in-law and his wife to inform them

of the situation. Dirk said he could definitely hack into Dad's security camera system. "Why don't you come over?" Dirk said. "I'll call Roger and Ronnie, and we can discuss this."

"Will do," Robin said. He hung up his phone and looked at me and Eddie. "Why don't you guys head over to Dirk and Lisa's. I'll get Brooke and met you there."

"Sure," I agreed. We left the house and headed to our separate modes of transportation. I decided to call Gunther again. I was sent straight to voicemail and all I could do was leave him a message. "Gunther, this is Queen Shelly. The king and I haven't heard from you all week and are very worried about you. I hope everything is alright. Please call us as soon as possible to let us know you are okay. Bye." I hung up and glanced at Eddie. "I'm really worried about Gunther. He's not one to flake out at his job."

The vampire nodded in agreement. "We should have someone check on him."

"But I don't want just anyone to show up at his house. He's an extremely private person. Do you remember when we picked him up one time? He met us at his door and didn't invite us into his house. At first, I thought he was just in a hurry, but now as I think about it, it was more like he didn't want us inside at all."

"There is definitely something he doesn't want us to know."

"I'll see if Cassius knows someone who can check in on him." My husband nodded in agreement. I called the airship captain and asked him to send someone over to check on the satyr. Cassius said he would get it done, but something in the tone in his voice told me he was hiding something.

Eddie started up the motorcycle, and we headed to my sister-in-law and brother-in-law's house. As we drove, I noticed a flash of silver out of the corner of my eye. I glanced over my shoulder but saw nothing. Using my heightened vampire senses, I quickly scanned the area for a heat signature or shallow breathing. Nothing. The rest of the ride was uneventful.

Chapter Five:

Ambushed at the In-Laws

My sister-in-law, Lisa Van Helsing, greeted us at the door of the green. Her green eyes widened the moment she saw the sword hanging from my side. The vampire's platinum blond hair was pulled back in a perfect, complicated braid. Now that my childhood friend was a vampire, I could read her mind. She saw something dangerous, yet calm in me. Like a warrior queen.

I walked up confidently and gave her a hug. "Hey, Lisa!"

"Shelly, it's good to see you." Lisa put her hands on both my shoulders and took a long, hard look with her grass-green eyes at my belt full of weapons. "You're armed?"

"Yeah, Eddie and I are a king and queen, and we kind of need to be armed."

"Well, you'd be the one to save our parents."

"Dirk tell you?" I asked.

Lisa nodded. "It never occurred to me that Dad and Libby had gone missing. We just assumed they were on sabbatical." Even as she said it, she knew in her heart that our fathers and stepmothers would never leave without telling anyone their whereabouts. " I just hope they are okay."

"Me too."

My husband and I followed Lisa inside to the living room where her husband, Dirk, had his laptop hooked up to their television. Dirk was only a few years older than Eddie and has the same green eyes, but the brothers were very different from each other. Dirk keeps his straight long black hair pulled back into a ponytail. He is also a strict pacifist and made a point about it when he saw our weapons. "Eddie, our home is a weapon-free zone!" He said by way of greeting.

My husband crossed his arms. "I can't remove my weapons. They are a part of my job."

Dirk raised an eyebrow. "As a king?"

"And a Guardian of the queen."

"A Guardian?" Lisa asked.

"My personal bodyguard," I explained.

Lisa's brother, Roger Miller, was sitting quietly on the couch with his supermodel girlfriend, Ronnie. "You two are royalty?"

"Shelly is the ruling queen of Peregrin. I'm only the king consort," Eddie explained.

They all looked skeptically at us, and I gave a Readers' Digest condensed version of how I became the queen of a hidden chain of islands and what brought us back to Zephyr. When I was finally done, Lisa asked. "So, you had a vision about our parents being enslaved, but you have no idea who is behind this or why?" She didn't believe I had visions, which is why I rarely tell people about them.

I didn't address her skepticism. "Pretty much. I think we might have a better idea when we watch the video feed." We heard a knock on the front door, and I volunteered to open it. I let my brother and his wife, Brooke, in.

My beaming, very pregnant sister-in-law gave me a hug. "It's good to see you, Shelly. Congratulations on your new job."

"Thanks," I said. My vampiric hearing suddenly picked up

two more heartbeats coming from Brooke. I wanted to ask her when she was due, but she beat me to it.

"I'm surprised Robin didn't tell you and Eddie," Brooke said. "We're having twins."

I gave a distracted smile as I saw a few flashes of silver out of the corner of my eye. I glanced around but received no feeling of danger. I still ushered both of them in the house. "Congratulations."

We all walked back to the living room, and I saw Eddie checking his cell phone. "Anything?" I asked him.

"Nothing. I'm tempted to have Dirk track his phone."

"No, that move would certainly invade his privacy."

Roger interrupted us. "Who are you guys are talking about?"

"It's my private secretary, Gunther. He took three personal days and was supposed to be at work today. He never showed up. Eddie and I can't get a hold of him. No one knows where he is. It's like he vanished without a trace."

"Maybe he quit," Lisa suggested.

"No! Gunther would never do that. Something happened

to him." Even though I can only read the minds of the undead, I could sense everyone's sympathy for us and our missing friend. "There's nothing that we can do here. Let's watch the video feed."

Dirk nodded. "All right, I've got it cued up to the day before we knew everyone was missing." He hit play. For the next few hours, we watched a typical day at Anderson's diner. Thank God, Dirk had it on high speed because I nearly fell asleep with boredom.

"Wait!" I shouted two hours later, waking everyone from their boredom.

Dirk paused the feed. "What?"

"Back it up a few minutes. I saw something."

Dirk did as I instructed, and we all watched the strange, horrifying scene unfold on the television.

My stepmother, Amelia Anderson looked up from her hostess' booth at the three men who had walked into the diner. "I'm sorry, gentlemen, but we're about to close."

The men shove her out of the way and barrel past her. Amelia tried to use her telekinesis to block their path with the hostess' booth, but one of them, a tall, thin man rushed at her with lightning speed.

I immediately recognized him as Jay Kramer, a lazy, rude detective on the Pembrook Police force. As I watched him on the screen, a memory resurfaced in my mind. It was at my mother's funeral. I had no idea why Kramer was there, but he was. I was sitting outside the church's steps, sobbing and not wanting to talk to anyone when he told me I shouldn't cry because my father would find someone to replace my mom.

Fortunately, Chris came outside and told Kramer to get lost. The detective called Chris an unkind word and went back inside.The dispatcher sat down beside me to comfort me.

Even though the bittersweet memory was over ten years old, I was still furious with Kramer. My hand gripped the hilt of my sword in anger. I didn't even realize I was slowly removing it from the sheath until I saw the terrified look on my family's faces. I quickly slid Knowledge back inside and dropped my arms to my side. I attempted to settle my anger as I continued to watch the video.

Kramer placed something around her neck and sped back to the group. Instantly a metal collar appeared around my stepmother's neck. We watched in shock as she tried to remove it with her mind, but her telekinesis didn't work. "This collar mutes your magical abilities," the man told her. He grabbed her shoulders and shoved her to her knees. Then he tied her hands behind her back with a zip tie.

"Timothy!" She screamed

My dad came running out of the kitchen, and the fast man subdued him before he could do anything. A collar similar to Amelia's appeared around my father's neck.

Dad struggled to remove the collar, but it seemed to tighten with each effort. Once his hands were tied, he was dragged next to Amelia. He knelt beside her and whispered something to her. When she nodded, he looked up at their attackers with shock and fear. "How did you get here?"

One of the men, an overweight detective with a smoker's voice sneered at my helpless father. Then he turned to gaze at my stepmother. "Who is this lovely lady?" He reached out to touch her cheek, but she nearly bit him.

"Don't touch my wife!" Dad snarled at him.

"A new one, huh? Where's your buddy, Detective Miller? I understand he survived the shootout." When Dad refused to answer, the man glanced at the speedster. "Find Miller and bring him back here."

The other detective ran out of the camera's view. Within seconds, he brought back Bruce and Libby Miller. Both had the same collars around their necks, and their hands were tied behind their backs. He shoved them hard to the ground. "It looks like

Miller got himself a new wife, too,"

"Are your kids around, Anderson?" Madison asked casually.

"No, they were killed in the house fire." Dad's lie seemed to slip off his tongue as if he has practiced it over and over. He glanced over at Bruce. "Bruce's kids are dead, too."

"He's telling the truth," Bruce added. A trickle of blood ran down his red mustachioed lip. "They were both killed in that shootout Mallory orchestrated."

"Good. This will make things easier." Kramer replied.

"Are you going to kill us?" Dad demanded.

Detective Gregory Madison gave a phlegmy cough before responding. "I wish, but Murad and Mallory want you to work in the mines. The heavy-set detective cracked his knuckles. "But he never said anything about you arriving a little beat up.”

We all winced and turned our heads as Madison began to beat Dad and Bruce senseless with his bare hands. Fortunately, the beatings ended when a black portal was opened up in the middle of the restaurant. Both Kramer and Madison dragged our unconscious fathers and our crying, but unhurt stepmothers through it. The black wormhole closed up and the restaurant was empty as a tomb.

“Shut it off,” I commanded Dirk.

My brother-in-law was taken aback by the rising anger in my voice but did as he was told. He shut it off the tv. “I had no idea.”

That was the breaking point. “No idea?” I yelled. “Did you guys even look for our parents? Or were you so stupid in thinking they just went on sabbatical?”

Before anyone could respond, I turned on my heel and headed out the front door. I stood on the little porch and didn’t realize how hard I was gripping the railing until I heard a crack beneath my hands. I stepped back and took a chunk of white wood with me.

The front door opened behind me and I heard my husband step out onto the stoop. "I don't think Dirk and Lisa will appreciate the wanton destruction of their property." He came over and placed an arm around me. "Want to talk about it?"

"I'm angry at the fact that someone has kidnapped Dad and Amelia, and no one even looked into their sudden disappearance." Eddie was about to say something, but I continued my rant. "No one told me that they were gone. I would've launched a full-blown investigation."

"With the non-existent police force of Peregrin?" Eddie asked.

I sighed. "Good point. I just wish I could find out about these things the old-fashioned way, like communication with my family. Not some random vision." I stopped suddenly as I heard clattering on the roof above us. I stepped off the porch and glanced upwards.

Three silver boned creatures were crouching on the edge of the roof. My vision had done them no justice. They were scarier in real life. It looked like someone had skinned them leaving only silver bones and the muscles connecting the joints. They had no faces, but I understood their intentions clearly as they brandished their double-bladed battle axes made from the bones of their fallen comrades. That's one creepy way to honor someone.

I barely had time to ponder this interesting turn of events because all three of the creatures decided to jump at me. I quickly activated my shield bracelet and threw one of the bone creatures onto the ground as it launched itself on my shield.

Eddie vaulted over the railing with his war scythe slicing the second creature in half. "You know how you were just talking about the need for communication?" The vampire activated his shield bracelet as he ran up next to me.

"Very funny, dear," I replied, whipping Knowledge from its sheath. I decapitated the third one before it tried to plunge a battle-ax into me. The odd thing about these creatures was the lack of blood. I felt like I was cutting through pliable metal, not muscle and tissue. I pressed my back against Eddie's back and was about to announce we were bone creature-free. I saw one more rushing at me. "I've got another one of these things coming at me head-on," I told him.

"I've got two coming at me from both sides."

Someone opened the door, and my family stood in the doorway. "Are you guys going to come out and help us?" I yelled.

"I'm unarmed, and Brooke doesn't want to harm the babies," Robin unhelpfully informed. Dirk and Lisa didn't have to give an explanation for their pacifism. Roger and Ronnie just stood there shell-shocked. One thing was clear: they were all amazed at me and my husband's combat skills.

"Be helpful or get back inside!" I ordered them. Once they went back inside, I said to Eddie. "Looks like it's just us."

"Three against two. It's not fair for these guys," Eddie said as he cleaved another bone creature in two with his scythe. "Make that two against two."

"At least I'm fulfilling the prophecy about being a warrior queen," I remarked as I rammed my shield into another bone creature. "We need one alive to find out where Dad and Amelia are."

"On it!" He rammed the last one with the butt of his shield. The creature slumped to the ground motionless. We looked down at it as we lowered our shields and put away our weapons. "I can't tell if it's breathing or not."

I shrugged. "Don't look at me. I know nothing about their anatomy." The creature stirred. "I'll get the arms."

"I'll get the legs," Eddie said. We lugged the unconscious creature to the porch stoop and dropped him unceremoniously on the ground. "Let's secure him before he wakes up."

I went inside and asked Dirk for some rope.

"Uh-uh, yeah. I think we have some in the garage," my shocked brother-in-law said. "Where did you and Eddie learn to fight like that?"

"Hours and hours of practice and life experiences," I replied as I headed into the garage.

"Shelly," Robin asked, "what are you guys doing with that thing?"

"Well, when it comes to, we're going to get some answers."

"How?" Lisa asked. "You're not going to hurt him?"

"No, nothing's going to happen to it," I said as I opened a drawer in a red toolbox, "but we need answers if we're going to find our parents. This is the only way." I closed the drawer and opened a second one. I grabbed a coil of rope and jogged back outside.

Eddie had the creature sitting up against the stoop. He expertly tied both its hands and feet, and the two of us waited for the thing to wake up. Fortunately, we didn't have to wait that long as it opened its eyes about ten minutes later. My husband began the interrogation. "Who do you work for?" he demanded. The thing only smiled showing its needle-like teeth.

"What happened to the owners of Anderson's?" Eddie asked.

"Gone, all gone. Hotel, gone." The creature replied in a raspy, sing-song voice. Then it moved its red tongue around its mouth for a few seconds before placing a small capsule between its teeth.

Eddie knew exactly what was about to happen. "Get down!" he ordered everyone as he threw me to the ground. He didn't have any time to activate his force field spell before the small explosion.

I was peppered with bits of silver bone and rubbery

muscle. My ears were ringing, and my head was pounding.

Eddie had shielded me with his body and was covering his ears. "You okay, babe?" he asked as he got up from the ground.

I nodded. "I think so. What was that?" I asked as I took his extended hand and pulled myself to my feet. Something wet ran down the side of my face. I touched it, realizing it was blood.

"A sonic capsule. Similar to a cyanide capsule--." He stopped quickly and caught me as I staggered back. "You're experiencing the side effects. We need to get you laying down."

I could barely register what the vampire was saying as another wave of dizziness swept over me. My legs felt like wet noodles as they gave away. I heard him say "I've got you, babe" as he scooped me up in his arms and carried me inside the house.

Inside I could hear even more concerned voices, but Eddie's was the only one I wanted to hear. I tried to open my eyes, but it hurt. I tried to send a telepathic message to Eddie, but my brain ached. My husband said something about letting me lay down somewhere quiet. I felt him carry me in a dark room and laid me down.

"I'm going to take off your weapons so you can be more comfortable."

I managed a nod as he removed my weapons belt. It hurt to move my head. I slowly laid on the bed

"Lie still, Shell," he whispered. "I'll be right back with something to help ease the headache."

I nodded as I slowly let sleep consume me.

Matt wheels through the open door of a darkened room. The door locks and seals behind him encasing him in darkness. "Hello?" He calls. "Is anyone here? I'm Matt Turner. I'm here for the consultation."

"Welcome, Mr. Turner." A disembodied voice echoes through the room. The lights flicker, and a man with red, blood-like skin appears n front of him. His black skull-like head is engulfs in bright orange flames. He swiftly injects a syringe filled with a dark liquid into the man's neck. Then everything goes dark.

I woke up with a start with a damp face cloth against my forehead. I felt around the bed and was relieved to touch my husband's hand.

"Did you have another bad vision?" Eddie asked me.

"Yeah. How could you tell?"

"You were thrashing around and mumbling about someone named Matt. One of your dad's friends, I assume."

I swallowed hard as I managed to sit next to him. "It's the same dream I had the days before he disappeared."

"Do you want to talk about it?"

I leaned into him as he put his arm around me and I told him about the dream. "I didn't tell anyone when I was first having the dream because I knew they wouldn't believe me. In Pembrook, you'd become a laughing stock if you told people you had psychic visions." I paused. I wasn't going to feel sorry for myself for not telling anyone about Matt's disappearance because this time, I was going to do something about it. "We do know one thing. That creature might be connected to all the missing people." I slowly started to get out of bed.

"How are you feeling?" Eddie asked.

"Much better, thank you. My head doesn't hurt, and my ears aren't ringing anymore. What happened to me?"

"We were hit with a sonic capsule. Prisoners sometimes use them to kill themselves before giving out any information to the enemy. It will cause the person's head to explode, but delivers a sound that will mess up their enemy's equilibrium."

"How come you weren't affected?"

"Once I realized what it was, I managed to plug my ears." He got up off the bed and retrieved both our weapons belts. "You've been asleep for about an hour. Robin, Brooke, Roger, and Ronnie have all gone home. They said to call with the next step when you get up."

"With what? The only information we got from the bone creature was the word 'Hotel.' Not a lot to go on."

"I'm sure you have a plan."

I shook my head. "I don't know where to go from here."

Eddie held up his hands. "Wait a minute, we have quite a bit of information."

I looked at him blankly. "Explain."

"First, we know that people with disabilities have been

disappearing from Zephyr. I'm pretty sure that if we do some digging that there have been other places where people have vanished as well. Second, we have that symbol. Someone has to have seen it before. Third, and I was thinking about this while you're sleeping, there has to be a connection with that obnoxious pinging noise and the sonic capsule. They both have similar side effects: headaches and tiredness."

"Lights hurting your eyes?"

"Exactly!"

I smiled. "It's a start. Dr. Wandasen is supposed to be back from his vacation. Let's get back home to see if he can help us find the source of that pinging noise."

"Hopefully with one of his working inventions."

Chapter Six:

The Secret Life of Gunther Hornicus

After discussing the situation with our family, Eddie and I headed back to the Monte Carlo. They told us that they would meet us in Peregrin once they were all able to get some time off with their employers. I gave each one of the directions to Pergrin via air or boat.

Cassius greeted us as we boarded the airship. "How was your meeting with your parents, your Majesty? He asked me.

"They're missing," I replied.

"Missing?" The captain looked shocked. "What happened?"

Eddie and I proceeded to tell him everything that had transpired in the last several hours. "I think my dad started investigating these disappearances and got caught in the crossfire," I explained.

"Do you know who's behind this?" Cassius asked.

"No," Eddie said, "but I still have contacts from the Agency. They might know something." Soon after he was turned into a vampire, my husband was a spy for an international intelligence company known as the Agency. The company shares ties with no one and is able to work for anyone anywhere.

"Any lead helps." I took out my phone and searched for the picture of the strange triangular symbol. Once I found it, I showed it to the captain. "Have you ever seen this?"

"No!" The lie came out of the vampire's mouth too quickly as he recognized the symbol. He turned around and walked back to the bridge without saying another word to Eddie and I. He even purposely blocked his mind from my telepathic ability.

I looked at my husband who shared my concern. "What is going on here?"

"Is he still blocking your telepathy?" Eddie asked.

"Yes. He had seen this symbol before, but I don't understand why he won't tell us. Am I giving off a bad vibe or something?"

"No, but he definitely knows something." Eddie fished his phone out of his pants pocket. "I'm going to reach out to my contacts at the Agency to see if they know anything about these disappearances."

"Good idea." We began to walk to our room, but my stomach started growling. "I'm starving. I'm going to swing by the galley to grab something to eat. You want anything?"

"Get me a bowl of Leo's baked Mac and cheese and a soda, please."

Leo, the minotaur cook, makes a delicious baked Mac and cheese dish loaded with Parmesan cheese and garlic. Contrary to popular belief, vampires can eat garlic. Eddie and I will put it on almost everything. "Ooh, that sounds good. I'll get one for myself as well."

Once we parted ways, I headed to the kitchen. I was walking past the infirmary when I heard two heated voices behind the closed door. I paused when the symbol was mentioned by Cassius, the owner of one of the voices. Don't judge me, but I stopped to listen.

"Just tell the queen everything." The second voice belonged to Delilah, Cassius's wife.

"No! I'm not betraying my best friend!"

"Queen Shelly is a reasonable woman. I'm sure she will understand."

"You don't know that. None of the other royals have made the effort to change the law. Gunther has been through enough, and I won't betray his confidence and seal his death sentence."

I gasped inwardly. Cassius and Delilah were suddenly terrified of me. What law were they talking about? Why would Gunther have a death sentence over his head? Nothing was making sense. I stepped back away from the door and hurried to the kitchen.

A big, burly minotaur was behind the counter flipping some hamburgers over a stainless steel stove. "What can I get for you, your Majesty?" He asked.

"Could I get two servings of your baked Mac and cheese and two sodas, please?"

"Sure thing, your Majesty. I've already pre-made some for you and the king."

I smiled. "Ah, you know us well." I decided to show him the symbol. "Leo, have you ever seen anything like this?"

"Oh, sure, I have. Mr. Hornicus showed me something similar about a year or so ago."

I raised my eyebrows in surprise. "Really?"

"Yep, he was showing it to everyone on the ship. I told him I had never seen it before.

"Even Cassius saw it?"

The cook nodded as he removed a glass pan filled with my food from the refrigerator and set it on the counter before getting two bowls and a serving spoon from a nearby cabinet. He scooped out two servings in each bowl and placed it in the microwave. "It'll just take a few minutes to heat up. Unfortunately, Mr, Hornicus never told me why he was looking for the symbol. Is he in some sort of trouble?" When the microwave beeped, Leo took out the bowls and placed covers on them. He placed them carefully in plastic shopping bags along with two sodas along with four chocolate fudge cookies.

"Not at all. Just trying to figure out what this symbol means." I put my phone away and took the bag from him.

"Thanks for everything, Leo."

"You're welcome, your Majesty. I hope you figure out what that symbol means. I don't think Mr. Hornicus ever did."

I nodded in agreement and waved good-bye to the minotaur. I walked back to our room, bravely resisting the temptation to eat all of the delicious cookies. Eddie had just finished up his phone call when I walked. "Did you find anything out?" I set our meal on the table.

"Yes and no," he answered as he opened up the bag and set out the food. "My contacts told me they have been investigating the disappearances for almost 20 years. They have traced it to someone called the Mannequin King."

I retrieved two forks from a tiny drawer in the kitchenette. "The guy we saw opening the black portal?"

"They don't know what this guy looks like. Most of the information the Agency has gotten on him are unsubstantiated rumors. No one has been able to identify him and lived to tell about it."

"So what does this guy do?"

Eddie took a bite from one of the cookies. "No one knows

for sure. He abducts people, but no one knows why. This Mannequin King is excellent at covering his tracks but uses the same M.O. we have seen."

I want to be healthy, so I started to eat the macaroni and cheese dish first. After taking a few bites, I said. "I guess that's somewhat helpful."

"Sorry, babe. Even though I no longer work for them, I felt they were telling me all that they knew."

"Another complication," I told him about the conversation between Cassius and Delilah and my talk with Leo. "I don't understand why nobody is telling us anything."

"Maybe Gunther's involved with this Mannequin King, and Cassius is protecting him."

"Oh, Cassius is protecting him all right, but from something else entirely. We need to get to the bottom of this as soon as possible."

We landed back home and were confronted by the Minister of Science and Technology, Dr. Wandasen. The short, plump wizard apparently had pacing outside my office for quite a while as I could see a worn pattern on the carpet. He pulled his tinfoil hat over his ears as he leaned in to whisper to me. "They have landed, your Majesty!"

"Who has landed?" I asked.

"The aliens."

Eddie and I briefly exchanged looks. "When did they land?"

"Several weeks ago. They have hidden their ship underground so that we can't find it."

"But how do you know they have landed?"

The scientist scoffed at me as if I was the one sporting a tinfoil hat. "Their spaceship makes loud pinging noises that can be heard throughout the entire queendom."

As paranoid as the wizard was, he was onto something. I had an idea. "Do you think you can locate the spaceship so that the king and I can stop the invasion?"

Dr. Wandasen's eyes became big as terrified saucers. "I don't want them to find me!"

"The king can help you rig up an invisibility cloak or something," I suggested.

Eddie shot me a look. *Why are you pulling me into this? This is your brilliant idea.*

Because we need Dr, Wandasen to pinpoint that pinging noise. I'm sure you have some sort of invisibility gadget from your spy days.

I used stealth, not invisibility. My husband sighed reluctantly. "Dr. Wandasen, we can go down to the armory to see if there is anything you can use to conceal yourself."

"I have a sonar device I can set up," Dr. Wandasen said reluctantly. "All right, I'll do it as long as the aliens can't see me."

"You'll be doing a great thing for the queendom," I assured him. I watched as the inventor and the king walked towards the armory. I hoped against hope I was doing the right thing.

A tall, aging centaur was walking towards me. "Your Majesty, shall I have the kitchen prepare a meal for you and the king?" He asked with a bow.

"No, thanks, Rupert. Eddie and I ate on the way here" I decided to show my butler the symbol. "Have you ever seen this before?"

He nodded. "Yes, Mr. Hornicus was asking about that

same symbol two years ago.”

“Do you know why?”

“No, he never told me. But he did tell me it could have belonged to someone named the Mannequin King. I surmised Mr. Hornincus was trying to locate him. I remember he was asking Cassius and me about it that day.”

Cassius had been lying to me all along. I needed to talk to him and get to the bottom of this whole mess. I thanked Rupert for his help and excused myself into my office. After closing the door, I called Cassius on my cell phone. “I know Gunther spoke to you about the symbol,” I told the airship captain once he had picked up and exchanged pleasantries with me. “I need to know why you’ve been hiding it from me.”

“Gunther’s personal life is none of your concern, your Majesty,” Cassius’ voice became very protective. “He wasn’t doing any of this on work time, I can guarantee you that. What he does on his own time should not concern you.”

“Do you know where he is?”

“No, your Majesty. I haven’t heard from him since he last talked to you and the king.”

"You never checked in on him?"

"I called him, but he never answered his phone."

"Okay," was all I could muster. I was blown away by the vampire's harsh response and the mounting piles of lies that were unraveling.

I heard a knock on my office door. "Shell, I'm back," I heard my husband say from the opposite side of the door. I opened it and beckoned him inside. "Eddie and I are going to check in on him right now." I hung up the phone.

"What's going on?" Eddie asked.

I gave him a summary of what I learned as we headed out to the courtyard where Eddie stores his cars and his motorcycle. "What really angers me is that no one has done a wellness check on Gunther. He could be hurt and needs help."

Eddie nodded as he wheeled the motorcycle out of the mini-garage. "Cassius has always been very forthcoming with us. It doesn't make any sense that he would suddenly stop." He took out both of our helmets from the storage box on the bike's back and put his on before getting on

"That's why we are going to Gunther's to find out why," I

said as I buckled the chinstrap on my helmet. "By the way, did you find something for Dr. Wandasen in the armory?"

"You are very lucky there was an invisibility ring in there."

I gave him a grin as I climbed behind him. "To think you doubted me."

Eddie smirked as he started the motorcycle. The engine roared to life, and we raced off the castle grounds to our private secretary's house.

Gunther lives in a three-story, teal, single-family detached house with a back porch overlooking the ocean. Eddie turned into the well-maintained driveway and turned off the bike. The first thing he noticed was the opened oak front door as we dismounted the motorcycle. He took out his war scythe from his belt clip and extended it to its full length.

Knowledge was already in her sword form, and all I had to do was to withdraw it from the sheath. I followed my husband to the front porch and watched as he peered in the opened doorway. Using all of my vampiric senses, I determined that there was no one there. "He's not here.

"Even so," Eddie said, " Stay close." He walked in first with me right behind. "I'll search upstairs if you want this floor."

The front door opened up into a small beige hallway. At the end was an almost immaculate living room with brick-red painted walls. There was a dark green leather sectional couch surrounding an antique glass coffee table cluttered with papers and balled-up tissues. A flat-screen television hung over a fireplace.

There were five framed pictures sitting on the mantle. Three of them were black and white photographs of what I assumed were Gunther's relatives and one of him sitting in a fishing boat as he unraveled a net. The fifth one that was almost pushed back to the wall caught my attention.

It was a more recent photograph of a grinning Gunther sitting on a rocky beach with a faun next to him. The smiling half-man, half-sheep was holding the satyr's hand. The faun looked similar to the satyr, except for his two black wooly, sheep-shaped legs and the curling horns on both sides of his head. The faun sported a pair of dark-rimmed glasses that brought out his blue eyes.

The kitchen and dining area were just as immaculate. Black marble lined the countertops to match the stainless steel appliances. The only non-modern item was the round retro 1950s white table with four red cushioned chairs. It looked really great there. I found a picture of Gunther with the same faun on the refrigerator. This one had been taken on one of the couches in the living room with them sitting together with their arms around each other and laughing. I had never seen my private secretary look so happy before.

"Found anything yet?"

I whirled around to face my husband. "Geeze, Eddie! You scared me!"

"Sorry about that." He glanced at the picture on the fridge. "He's got a few more pictures of him and that guy upstairs, even one of them kissing. Did you know Gunther has a boyfriend?"

"No, but they look very happy together. I wonder if he knows where Gunther is." I took the picture off the fridge and looked at the back. It was dated six years ago but gave us no names or anything.

"He doesn't, your Majesty."

Eddie and I turned around to find Cassius standing in the kitchen, his hands stuffed deep into his pants pockets. "Are you sure?" I asked.

Cassius nodded solemnly. "Yes, your Majesty. Enoch Bighorn died unexpectedly. Monday was the third anniversary of his death."

"Oh, no! Poor Gunther."

"He was devastated by Enoch's death. Gunther asked me about that symbol about a year after Enoch had died. I believe it has something to do with his death, but Gunther refused to tell me what, and I didn't ask."

"Cassius, why didn't you tell us this earlier?" Eddie asked. "We could've done something."

"Because I didn't want Gunther executed! He's a good man and has done nothing wrong."

I gave the airship captain a shocked look. "Why would he be executed?"

"You don't know about the law, do you?" Cassius asked hesitantly.

"What law?" Deep in my gut, I was afraid of the answer,

but I steeled myself.

"It is illegal to be gay here in Peregrin and is punishable by public execution."

The answer hit me like a ton of bricks as my hand flew up to my mouth. Everything I knew about Gunther started to fall into place. Him not telling me and Eddie about his personal life, Cassius' fierce protection of him. Even the few pictures of Gunther and his boyfriend made sense. The satyr was terrified of being found out. Then shock overcame me. "That's barbaric!"

I looked over at my husband who was seething at the terrible injustice. "It's not only barbaric but discriminatory. How many people have died under this so-called law?" He asked Cassius.

"I've lost count over the years, sire."

"This ends now," I said. "I will not tolerate any kind of discrimination under my rule, especially ones so barbaric. People should not have to live in fear because of who they love. I'm changing this law." I inadvertently read Cassius' mind and knew he was so relieved to learn about Eddie and my acceptance of Gunther's sexuality, but he was worried about the consequences of his actions. "You're not in any trouble, Cassius. You were just trying to protect Gunther. He's lucky to have a good friend like you."

"Thank you, your Majesty. Only Delilah and I know about Gunther being gay, and now you two. When you find him, please let me tell him."

Eddie and I nodded in agreement. "Of course," my husband said. "Did Gunther ever mention to you about someone named the Mannequin King?"

"Yes, when he first showed me the symbol, he kept blaming someone named the Mannequin King for Enoch's death. I tried to reason with him, but Gunther was so overcome with grief I assumed he wasn't seeing things straight. Why do you ask?"

Eddie quickly told him what he learned from the Agency. "Looks like Gunther was onto something."

I was getting uncomfortable standing uninvited in my private secretary's kitchen. "Let's get out of here." Once we were outside, I turned to the airship captain. "I need you and your crew to be on standby. We'll leave as soon as we get a solid lead on my parents and Gunther's whereabouts."

Chapter Seven:

A Solid Lead Literally Drops in

Eddie and I had barely stepped into our office when a red-headed genie in her late thirties rushed in. She wore a flowered sleeveless shirt, black pants, and black pumps. "I need to talk to you, your Majesty." She wasn't demanding, but really concerned about something very urgent.

I sat down at my desk with Eddie standing behind me. "Have a seat," I said as I gestured toward one of the chairs. Once she was sitting down, I asked, "What can I do for you?" She took a deep breath. "My name's Marcie, and I need your help. I'm a journalist for an online newspaper here in Peregrin and for the past several years I have been looking into the disappearances of some of your very own citizens. I heard about your investigation and thought we could compare notes."

Eddie and I glanced at each other, wondering if this would be connected to our family's disappearance. "Who told you?"

"A woman named Colleen Macaw. She contacted me via email saying that she had information about my investigation." Eddie crossed his arms over his chest. "Have you ever met this woman?"

"Of course, we met at Cold Stone Coffee. She told me you and the queen were investigating the disappearance of a man named Walter Tibias."

I raised a suspicious eyebrow. Eddie and I had never told anyone, except for our family, about the missing Minotaur. "How did she come across this information?"

"You told her personally," Marcie answered.

I was about to contradict her when my husband interrupted me. "Please describe this woman."

Marcie looked at us with uncertainty in her gray eyes. "Okay, she's a Winged One with blue and gold wings, about the same height and built as the queen. Oh, she also had long black hair that sparkled."

I nodded, but my mind raced. The other Colleen had the

same type of hair, but she was a minotaur. What were we dealing with? I knew Eddie was thinking the same, but I didn't want to scare off Marcie. "Tell us about your investigations."

She eyed me. "Wait a minute. Why are you asking so many questions about Colleen Macaw?"

I didn't want to give away our suspicions. "We would like to tell her the information we found about her brother," I lied.

Marcie evidently decided to ignore my blatant lie. "About ten years ago, a genie couple named Fred and Paula went into a brand-new medical treatment center in hopes of curing Fred's paralysis. They were never heard from again." She choked on the last few words as tears filled her eyes.

I sighed inwardly. I had heard this story way too many times already. But this was obviously very personal for her."You knew them, didn't you?"

"Yes, your Majesty, they were my brother and sister-in-law. Before you ask if they just decided to skip town, the answer is no. They would never leave their son. I've been raising Elliot on my own since he was three."

I nearly bolted from my chair in outrage. This kidnapper

had broken up a family and left a kid parentless. My mother died when I was thirteen, and I still miss her every day. I couldn't imagine the pain of losing both Mom and Dad at the same time or not knowing if they were still alive. I showed her the symbol on my phone.

Shock washed over her. "That's the same symbol that was at their house!"

I nodded. "My father and stepmother have gone missing as well as two of their friends. We discovered this symbol in their houses."

"Marcie," Eddie asked, "has your research ever turned up someone named the Mannequin King?"

"No, who is he?"

"We don't know, but we think he is somehow connected to all these disappearances." I saw the thoughtful look in my husband's eyes and knew he had an idea. He described the strange creature with the burning head to the genie.

That got a reaction. "You guys saw a portal devil?" Her bluish-purple skin flushed an angry red hue

"What's a portal devil?" I asked. I knew about demons,

had even battled a low-level one, but never heard of portal devils.

"My people," Marcie said, "are from another plane of existence called Wishteria."

"People can only get there by opening wormholes," I said.

"Yes, how did you know?"

"I knew a genie named Abbott. Go on."

"There is only one other being on Wishteria." Marcie went to tell the long history of her homeland. Portal devils love to trick people into making unbreakable, lifetime deals. They thrive on hate and evil. Genies and portal devils have been battling each other on Wishteria for millennia. She paused as tears filled her eyes. "If Fred and Paula encountered a portal devil, they may already be dead."

"Whatever the outcome, Eddie and I will inform you," I assured her. I didn't want to give her false hope as she already had lost so much. I was about to ask her if she had any idea where the portal devil might be hiding when we heard a loud commotion outside.

The three of us rush to the gardens through the sliding

door in my office. Gunther's nephew, a satyr in his twenties, was standing over the body of a blond-haired man in torn, bloodied clothing. The gardener had dropped his trimming shears and had a look of pure shock and confusion on his face. A tall green version of Chewbacca was snarling at the prone man with bloodlust in his eyes.

He was about to lunge forward. I had to stop him before he tore the body apart. "Harvey! Stop!" I ordered. The plant creature froze in place but kept snarling. I knew he had gone into self-preservation mode. The self-proclaimed protector of the gardens had been startled somehow.

Eddie knew exactly what could calm Harvey down. He raced back inside. Within minutes, the vampire was back with an opened can of Vienna sausages. He took out one and tossed it away from the scene. The green man chased it after like a dog. Eddie tossed a few more to keep Harvey at a safe distance until he calmed down.

"What's going on?" I asked the shaking Jake. The satyr shook his horned head. "I was just trimming the bushes here. Suddenly this guy appeared out of nowhere." He pointed to the man who we could now tell was breathing shallowly. "Like, one second, he wasn't there. Then, like POOF! He was there. He nearly scared the crap out of me! Then Harvey started charging over here."

"Was anyone hurt?" I asked.

"No, but this guy could be."

I crouched down to take the man's pulse and immediately recognized him. Matt Turner looked like he was in his twenties, but the last time I saw him, he was at least ten years older. I noticed circular bruising patterns around his neck, hands, and ankles. Half of his t-shirt was so torn that I could see long, deep scarring across his back. What had happened to him?

Matt moaned as he slowly came to. "Where am I?" He asked. His dry lips cracked and bled as he spoke. "Fred? Paula?"

Eddie was about to help him to his feet when I stopped him. "He can't walk. He's paralyzed from the waist down!"

"No! I can walk. I'm cured." Matt attempted to stand, but his legs collapsed under him as if they were wet spaghetti. Both Eddie and Marcie caught him before he fell to the ground.

"He lied! He frigging lied to me!" Matt said in despair.

"Matt, how bad are your injuries?" I asked.

Matt finally looked me in the eye. "Who are—Shelly Anderson?" I thought—."

"I'll explain later," I said hastily. "How bad are your injuries? Can we move you?"

He took a deep breath to compose himself and winced in pain. "A couple of my ribs and my right shoulder might be broken. I don't know if there are any other injuries."

"Okay." I looked at my husband. "Do you think you can move him inside?"

Eddie nodded. "I'm not sure how we'll be able to transport him, Shell."

"Here, let me help," Marcie said. A tattoo of a butterfly emerging from a cocoon began to glow brightly on her left arm. Moments later, we all watched as the genie transformed into a purple centaur. She knelt down her forelegs and assisted us as we helped Matt onto her back. "You know Fred and Paula?" she asked him.

"Knew," Matt said as one of his hands wavered in a failed

attempt to steady himself when she got to her feet. He obviously didn't want to grab anything without her permission.

"Here," Marcie said as she turned her torso around to face him. She gently held his hands and put them around her. "Wrap your arms around me so you don't fall off."

"Thanks," Matt replied painfully with gritted teeth.

"Jake, call Delilah and tell her to bring her medical kit," I ordered the young satyr.

The gardener nodded and ran back inside. We were about to follow him when I saw a black hole literally open up about 100 feet in front of us. Three dozen bone creatures emerged from it before the hole vanished and began to advance towards us.

Matt looked horrified as he clearly recognized them. "Shelly, these things are dangerous. You need to get somewhere safe. They will kill you."

I activated Truth with a push of a button. The metal shield popped up on my forearm. "Not if we get them first," I said as I drew Knowledge from her sheath. I looked at Eddie. "You ready, hon?"

The vampire grinned at me as he activated his own shield bracelet. "Always, babe," he said as he withdrew Vengeance from his belt, and with a quick shake, extended the war scythe to its full deadly length.

The first barrage clearly wasn't expecting Eddie and I to be so skilled in hand-to-hand combat, as was Matt. We dispatched three of the silver creatures with our weapons in a matter of seconds.

"Is it wrong that I have 'Another One Bites the Dust' stuck in my head?" I asked my husband.

"Yes," Eddie said as he sliced away at the legs of the bone creatures, "because we're not singing it together."

We belted out a couple more lines of the iconic Queen song as we took out a few more attackers but soon realized that even Freddie Mercury couldn't help us as we began to tire from the battle.

"Your Majesties!" Marcie shouted from behind Eddie and I. "Get down!"

We immediately obeyed and fell to the ground. I had no idea what she was going to do, but the tone in her voice indicated we had better stay clear.

The genie's light gray eyes turned completely white as the cyclone-shape tattoo on her right forearm began to glow brightly. A tornado emerged from the palm of her hand. She shoved it off, and it steadily increased to a full-sized, spinning funnel cloud of death.

Eddie quickly activated a force field spell around the two of us. From the safety of the green force field, we watched in impressive horror as the tornado quickly gathered up the remaining bone creatures into the air. "Wow!" he said.

"Wow is right!" I said as the tornado instantly vanished leaving no other damage, other than dropping a pile of torn bone creatures in its wake."Note to self: Don't ever tick her off."

Eddie dissipated the force field. "That's some pretty impressive elemental magic."

She shrugged. "I'm a part-shapeshifting and part-elemental genie." We all went back inside to my office. Eddie and I helped Matt off her back which allowed her to transform back to her normal form.

By the time Matt was settled on the couch, Delilah had

arrived with her medical kit. The plump, vampiric doctor began to attend to the injured man with an x-ray pen she took out from her bag. Once she waved it all over his body, she put it away and instructed him to take off the remains of his shirt. "You're a very lucky man," she said to Matt as she retrieved a bottle of unicorn pills. "Three of your ribs and collarbone are broken, but none of your internal organs are punctured." She took out two of the pills and gave them to Matt.

"It didn't feel like that when Blinky attacked us," Matt muttered.

"Blinky?" Marcie seemed to recognize the name. "Are you referring to a manticore?"

Matt nodded solemnly. "He belonged to Fred and Paula."

"Blinky is very docile. He wouldn't hurt anyone, especially Fred and Paula." Marcie clasped her hands to her mouth. "That's what portal devils do," she whispered softly.

"Do what?" I asked.

"Turn our pet manticores against us."

Wow. Everything about this portal devil was pure evil. He needed to be stopped.

Matt looked suspiciously at the rainbow-colored, oval-shaped pills in his hand. "What are these?"

"Unicorn pills. They will heal you up in no time."

I got up from my desk chair and retrieved a paper cup filled with water from my private bathroom. I handed it to Matt. "Water helps them go down faster," I told him. "We have questions."

He shrugged as if taking unicorn pills was an everyday process. He downed both of them with the water. "So do I."

"Okay, I'll start." I gave my friend from Pembrook a brief summary of how I got to Peregrin, starting with my family's arrival in Zephyr to look for Dad and Amelia. "We don't know where they are."

After Delilah put his arm in a sling and left the castle, Matt began to tell his story. His kidnapper, Murad, had abducted him and forced him to work in his underground mine. The portal devil, the same one we had seen at the retirement home, had cast a spell on Matt (Eddie surmised it was an illusion spell) to make him and everyone around him think his paralysis was cured. The mine was procuring fake gems and selling them at the highest value.

Somehow, Murad recruited former Pembrook detectives, Greg Madison, Jay Krammer, and Chief James Mallory, to work for him. They could be as brutal and sadistic as they wanted without any consequences. About a month ago, my father, stepmother, the Millers, the Bakers, and Dusty Williams had been captured. Every one of the prisoners was placed in a collar that suppressed his or her magical abilities. Matt paused in his narration and looked at Marcie. "Your sister, brother-in-law, and I led a revolt. Paula was the one who started it. Unfortunately, Murad and his men crushed it very quickly." He swallowed hard. "Murad sent us to the manticore arena and forced Blinky to attack us. Paula and Fred didn't make it. My collar was broken off, and I somehow ended up here."

"You must have teleported," Eddie answered.

"How?"

"Every human who arrives in this world gains a magical ability," I explained. "I can communicate telepathically with the undead."

"But you're a vampire!"

"I've only been one less than a year," I replied. "Are my father and stepmother alive?"

"They were the last time I saw them."

I took a deep breath. "All right, where is this mine located?"

"Next to his casino."

"Which is?"

Matt shrugged and then remembered his broken collarbone. He winced. "I don't know. I don't even know the name of the casino." He looked crestfallen at me. "I'm sorry, Shelly. I wish I could be of more help."

"The good thing about being a queen is that I have resources. Plus, an insane amount of awesome research skills from my days as a library assistant." My cell phone beeped to indicate I had received a text message. The string of numbers confused me as I tried to decipher Dr. Wandasen's message. I showed it to everyone. "I think he may have located the source of the loud pinging noise, or maybe he is messaging me in code."

"Those are coordinates, Shelly," Eddie said. He got up

from leaning on my desk and went to his own desk. Once he got on his computer, he quickly plugged in the coordinates online. "Got it. The noises are coming from an underground hotel called the Lucky Diamond, owned by— and I quote—'the enigmatic A. Drum.' It's about fifty miles from here on one of Peregrin's uninhabited islands."

"An anagram for his name?" I said. "This guy's not as smart as he thinks is."

Marcie started to get angry. "We know where this guy is! Send the army after him!"

I shook my head. "Our military is still rebuilding, and I will not send an army to invade one of our citizens."

"You're going to do nothing?" Matt asked.

"No," I said as a very clever idea began to form in my head, "but I do think it is time for Eddie and me to take a vacation to the Lucky Diamond Hotel and Casino."

"So you and your husband can investigate what's going on and conduct a rescue mission?" Matt guessed.

I nodded.

Marcie looked at Matt. "I'll stay here with Mr. Turner and

make sure none of those creatures come after him again." I suspected it wasn't the whole truth. She most likely wanted to know more about what happened to her family. Then I noticed her blushing and quickly covering it up by not looking at him. Was she starting to like him?

"If that's what you want," I said. I called for Rupert to assist Matt into one of the guest suites on the floor above us. Once my butler had left with the healing man and the genie, I called both Robin and Lisa to tell them that we may have found where our parents were. They were very excited to hear the news and told me that it would take them about three hours to get here. I made an overnight reservation at the Lucky Diamond.

Then I called Cassius while Eddie went down to the armory to collect extra weapons. "We may have found the Mannequin King."

"How?" The vampire captain sounded astonished.

I gave a quick rundown of what had happened since I had seen him last. "Do you think you can have the *Monte Carlo* ready to leave in four hours?"

"Yes, your Majesty."

"Also, what is the name of that law?"

"It doesn't have a name. It's just called Article 84 Section 7.1." He recited the law with a pained voice hinted with anger. I wondered how many times he had heard it proclaimed throughout the years.

I jotted down the law because I knew myself all too well. I suck at numbers, and I wouldn't remember it unless I had it written down in my hands. "Do you know where I can find a copy of it?"

"We don't have copies of our laws, your Majesty. They are written down in several books. I believe they are stored in the royal vault."

"All right, thank you, Cassius. I'll see you in a few hours." I hung up my phone and sent Eddie a quick text about my plan before stuffing my phone into the back of my jeans before heading to the royal vault.

Chapter Eight:

I Discover Just How Evil My Ancestors Were

The royal vault is exactly what it sounds like: a vault. This particular one is about the size of a large shipping container built into Castle Delorean's wall on the bottom floor. There was a clipboard with a sign-in sheet next to the vault door. I had installed it along with a new security camera because of the incident with the stolen firestones. Even though the only people with access to the combination code was Eddie, myself, and Hiram, our prime minister, I still wanted a safety measure to keep myself and everyone honest. I signed the sheet with my name, date, time, reason, and signature before rotating and unlocking the thick reinforced turnstile combination lock on the steel door. Even with using all my vampiric strength, I still struggled with opening the door all the way. A smart security measure my ancestors had put in years ago. I opened the door wide enough for me to squeeze through. I wedged the large stone door stopper through the crack. The last thing I wanted was to be locked in the vault for who knows how long.

Turning on the vault's ancient string of single bulbs that lined the ceiling created dusty, broken shadows across the interior. Not particularly helpful if you're unfamiliar with the vault's layout. "Note to self," I said aloud, "replace the lights in here so people can actually find what they're looking for."

I turned on my flashlight app on my cell phone and began to search for the law books. I walked past the seven dull firestones in their even more secured impenetrable glass cases and the side walls lined with all the artifacts and artwork that would be placed in Peregrin's first history and art museums. The firestones had helped pay for the museums, construction as well as all the public library, zoo, aquarium, children's museum, sports stadium, theater, hospitals, schools, and many other buildings that were going to be either built or rebuilt to ensure Peregrin's growth as a constant growing civilized, cultured society.

I finally found the law books stuffed deep back in the back wall of the vault. The last light bulb must have burnt out ages ago. I pulled the first, large book off a middle shelf. A cloud of dust nearly choked me as I lifted the cover. In almost fading letters, the title read: *The Laws of Peregrin: Book 8 of 20.* I carefully opened up the ancient book and turned to the first page which was the table of contents. This book contained Articles 40-45. Well, that was no help at all. I needed Article 84, but I was curious about the other laws.

I began to skim through the first couple of pages. Most of them were outdated and absurd, such as no chewing gum on the tenth day of the month or not allowing dragons to sleep in a bathtub. I hefted the heavy book back in its place and looked at Book 9. It only had articles 46-50 and had more silly laws that were outdated, such as only two letters were to be mailed each day.

After going through a few more books, I finally got the hang of the system. Each book contained five articles handwritten by either the queen or a member of the cabinet. I didn't want to waste precious time skimming through the books, and I just looked at the table of contents of each one until I found the right one: Book 16 of 20. With the help of the table of contents, I found Article 84 Section 7.1.

Anger mixed with horror blossomed in my chest as I read the law aloud as if to convince myself that I was imagining the words. "A man shall not pursue or engage in an intimate relationship with another man. A woman shall not pursue or engage in an intimate relationship with another woman. Violation of this law is punishable by death by public execution. If a man or woman is caught or suspected violating Article 84 Section 7.1, both parties involved will be immediately brought to the town square for beheading."

That was all the law said. No judge. No jury. Just immediate unjust execution. How many people have died under this cruel law since its inception? Hundreds or even thousands? How many families had to watch their loved ones die a horrifying death?

I began to recognize the symptoms of a psychic vision overcoming me. First came the nausea and dizziness. I sank to my knees to prevent a dangerous fall and let the darkness wash over me.

I am standing in the middle of the town square, people pressing against me on every side. I look down at my clothing and realize I'm wearing similar clothes to everyone else, a drab tunic. My vision had sent me back in time to the middle ages. There is an uneasy silence amidst the crowd like the calm before the storm as everyone's eyes are focused on the stone platform. I look on in horror as the scene before me.

Two terrified elvin women are forced to their knees with their hands tied behind their backs as they face a large crowd. Standing off to the right is the Minister of Virtue and Morals, Doctor Vincent Orlock. The tall, arrogant vampire barely looks at the women with absolute disgust in his eyes before turning to the crowd. He looks at the scroll in his hands but since he has written the law, he reads it from memory. "Justine Elfstone and Sylvia Elfsin, you have violated Article 84 Section 7.1. The punishment for this is death by beheading." He puts away the scroll back into his robes and motions for a masked executioner

to begin. In one swift, ugly movement, the elf is beheaded.
Orlock ignores pleas and screams for mercy before watching the
second woman executed.

I wince as the elves' screams filled my ears and thoughts.
I want to scream at Dr. Orlock to stop this horrible act, but my
mouth feels like it's full of cotton and I feel like vomiting.

The world began to spin as time moved forward in my
vision. My clothing and the era changed, but the executions were
the same. Hundreds of men and women pleading for mercy to
the empty ears of Doctor Orlock. Every single one of my
ancestors looks on in disinterest at the injustice displayed
throughout the centuries.

"Shell, are you okay?"

I felt my husband's arms wrapped around me as I came
out of the vision. I managed to tell him about my horrific vision
before I buried my face into his chest. I began to weep for all
those people who had been murdered under this barbaric law all
because of who they loved. I mourned for my ancestors'
uncaring attitude and unwillingness to end this horrific

discrimination. All Eddie did was hold me in his arms. After a long time, I finally wiped the few remaining tears away before showing him the law.

A look of horror swept over Eddie's face. "Your ancestors let Dr. Orlock get away with this?" He asked.

I nodded as I wondered if this was what happened to Enoch. It would make sense why Gunther hated Dr. Orlock so much. "But not anymore. This ends now."

"You need to remove him from your cabinet. What he has done over the centuries is incomprehensible. Not only did Orlock orchestrate the death of all those innocent people, but he also did it without a trial. They never stood a chance," Eddie said.

"Oh, I intend to, but not until this law is abolished." I got to my feet and put away the law book before Eddie and I left the vault. My subjects deserved to feel safe in their own county.

The rest of my family arrived about two hours later. Eddie and I packed one overnight bag with both casual clothes and dress clothes we didn't care about. We wanted to give the portal devil an illusion of refinement, but our black dress suits were practical for combat as well.

We met them in the lobby of the castle. I smiled as they looked around in awe of what Eddie and I now owned. "Holy cow, Shelly! All of this belongs to you?" Robin asked.

"Yeah," I said as I led everyone to my office, "we're still in the process of redecorating. Mom's ancestors had a unique taste in style." Once everyone was inside, I shut the door and faced everyone. "Okay, here's the plan. Eddie and I have made reservations at the Lucky Diamond Hotel and Casino. We will be the only ones going to the hotel. I don't want the kidnappers to get suspicious if we all suddenly show up there."

Lisa wasn't convinced. "What if Chief Mallory or Detective Madison recognizes Shelly?"

"Murad, the owner, is expecting the queen and king of Peregrin, not Shelly Anderson," Eddie pointed out.

"Madison hasn't seen us in years. We've all changed, especially me. I will also be introducing myself as Queen Michelle," I explained.

Roger shook his head. "I still don't like it. I think Robin,

Dirk, Eddie, and I should be the only ones going. You ladies should stay here where it's safe."

I tried so hard not to roll my eyes. I appreciated his chivalry, but I knew I could take care of myself. Plus, the only other person I wanted to watch my back was my husband. "No, it will only be Eddie and me," I said. "I will not have anyone else get hurt."

"Okay," Roger said finally.

Ronnie said. "The rest of the girls will stay here."

"That's no problem," I replied. "I'll have the staff here set you up in some of our guest suites if you wish."

Eddie hefted a large suitcase onto my desk, nearly knocking off my computer, keyboard, and phone in the process. He unzipped it and showed the men our clothes.

"Thanks?" Robin asked.

Eddie only smiled as he reached around the bottom of the suitcase, and we all heard Velcro snapping off. He lifted up the bottom to reveal a hidden compartment. "Take your pick, boys."

My brother and brothers-in-law were impressed with the wide assortment of weapons the vampire had collected from the armory. Robin picked out a vaporizer gun. "Nice!"

Roger grabbed the other vaporizer. "Are these the latest models?" He asked.

"I think so," Eddie said. He looked at his brother. "You want one, Dirk?"

The other vampire shook his head vigorously. "You know how I feel about weapons, Eddie. I'd rather stay here with my wife."

"Okay," my husband. "Brooke, are you coming with us?"

Robin's wife shook her head. "No, I should stay here."

Eddie zipped up the suitcase and took it off my desk. "Are we ready?"

Everyone nodded.

"Then let's go rescue our parents," I said.

Chapter Nine:

How to Win Friends and Influence Portal Devils

The flight to Devil's Island was only an hour and a half long. I let Eddie give Robin and Roger a tour of the *Monte Carlo*. I had something very important to do. Once I was alone in our room, I pulled a pad of paper and a pen from a backpack I had brought with us. I began tapping the pen on the edge of the pad as I thought about what to name the new law. "Everyone needs to feel safe in Peregrin," I said aloud. "Everyone needs the same rights for life, love, and family." Then the title came to me. I wrote in big letters across the top of the page: The Equality Law. The wording of the law itself was next. For about fifteen minutes, I stared at the rest of the page. Writing laws was harder than I thought.

I decided to put together a bullet list of what I wanted to be included. Abolishment of Act 84 Section 7.1 would be the first thing to go. Marriage and adoption were also added to the list. I even added the wording "consenting adults" as a backup in case anyone tried to challenge me, especially Dr. Orlock. I began to write the law in full detail. Once I was done, I had to rewrite it about four more times. Five crumbled up pages later, I was satisfied with my work at last.

Eddie came into our room with two first aid kits. "I raided the infirmary with Delilah's help," he said as he put the plastic boxes in my backpack. "How did your writing session go?"

I handed him the final draft. "Read it yourself."

His green eyes read the paper as his head nodded in agreement. "This is fantastic, Shell. I had no idea you could write laws."

"Neither did I, but thank god for the good, old internet. I had to look up some of the legal wording to get it right."

"Great title, by the way."

I blushed. "Thanks, hon. Do you think it's going to work?"

Eddie nodded as he sat on the bed beside me. "I hope so." He reached out and took my chin in his hand. "God, you're so hot when you strive for justice!" He drew me close to him, and we kissed passionately for a few minutes until we heard the intercom buzz.

"We've arrived at the island, your Majesties," Cassius' voice boomed overhead.

I broke away from Eddie and hit the speaker button on the phone. "We'll be right there, Cassius." I quickly slipped the newly written law into the room safe away from prying eyes. I turned to look at my husband. "It's showtime."

Once we were transported to the rocky island, Eddie and I tested the comlinks in our ears to make sure they worked here. I could hear a faint buzzing sound coming from the background, and I wondered if it would get worse once we went underground.

Eddie looked around the barren, rocky land before us. "How are we supposed to find this place?"

I looked at the email from *Lucky Diamond* on my phone. "Apparently, we look for the rock that looks like a tree, and then we knock on the trunk twenty times."

"That seems excessive," Eddie said as he lifted up our Trojan suitcase's handle and began to drag it behind him as we started searching for the entrance to the hotel and casino.

I adjusted my backpack to distribute the weight. Knowledge was in her book form, and Vengeance looked like a golden stick. Both of our hidden weapons along with our utility belts were on top of the two first aid kits. The last thing we wanted was to alert Murad to our intentions.

Fortunately, the tree rock was only a few yards away and really easy to spot. If you weren't looking for it, you could mistake it for a large oak tree in a perpetual fall state. The thick trunk was wide enough for a car to drive through, and Eddie knocked the number of times required and rubbed his knuckles while a hidden door slid open. We had to shield our eyes from the extremely bright lights bouncing off the descending reflective stairs like pieces of a shattered mirror

I glanced around for a handrail but found none. This was

definitely dangerous. Potential guests would either meet their demise by blinding and then falling down the stairs or slipping on the stairs and watching themselves fall down. It was a lawsuit waiting to happen. Hugging the wall and thoughts and prayers would only help us as we walked down the stairs.

When we got to the bottom, we were greeted by a huge open area that had been hued out the rock. Right smack in the middle was our destination. The Lucky Diamond Casino and Hotel was basically a glamourized Motel Six. Behind the three-story casino and hotel was a barely visible tunnel leading deeper into the sea cave. "That must be where Murad is keeping his prisoners," I said as I pointed out the tunnel.

"Looks like it," Eddie agreed as we walked closer to the entrance.

I adjusted an imaginary bow tie. "Time to act like royalty." The enormous pink and gold neon sign flashed erratically above the gold-framed glass revolving doors in a failed attempt to welcome visitors. If the steps didn't assault our vision, then the lobby's interior certainly did the job. Multi-colored geometric shapes fought for dominance against the highlighter yellow shag carpet scheme. The walls were lined with thick, vertical bright pink and green stripes that went from floor to ceiling. The only subdued color in the place was the white cathedral ceiling.

"Colorful," Eddie observed.

"You'd think with all the money coming into the place, they would invest in a classier décor." My eyes wandered to the artwork lining the walls. A piece of me died inside when I saw beautiful nature scenes in watercolor that had been placed in rhinestone-studded frames. "Who put this color scheme together? Dopers?"

We made our way to the front desk which was painted gold and studded with precious gems. A young girl no older than twelve was sitting behind it. She had black hair tinted with natural red highlights and hazel eyes. Her name tag read Jenny.

"Welcome to the Lucky Diamond!" she said in a well-rehearsed voice. "What can I do for you?" She absentmindedly tugged at the steel collar around her neck.

I recognized Jenny Baker immediately and fought the urge to tell her that we had come to rescue her. The creepy mannequin dressed in a standard security uniform was keeping an unflinching and unblinking eye on her every move squelched that. "We're just checking in," I told her. "I am Queen Michelle, and this is my Guardian."

She quickly logged on to her computer and pulled up our reservation. "Yes, you are in our exclusive honeymoon suite on this floor. Room 148." She gave us a small envelope with two keys before hopping off the chair she was sitting in. "Let me show you to your room." She came around the desk and attempted to take the suitcase from Eddie.

I've got it," Eddie told her.

Jenny seemed confused as to what to do next. I decided to jump in. "But you can certainly show us to our room."

The girl nodded and quickly walked with us. I noticed her guard trailing behind us. I wished Knowledge was easily accessible in case the living mannequin decided to attack. I casually put myself between Jenny and the creature. "Aren't you a little young to be manning the front desk of a hotel and casino?" I asked her.

"It's better than working the mines."

"Mines?" Eddie asked.

Her hands flew up to her mouth as if she had spoken out of turn. Her eyes traveled up to the row of multiple security cameras lining the walls as we made a left turn down a long hallway. She said nothing more as she pointed to our door. Once the door was opened, she said in a fearful tone, "Mr. A. Drum would like to have you for dinner." She hurried off before Eddie and I could offer her a tip.

I shut the door. "I know her. That's Andrew and Natalie Baker's daughter, Jenny."

"That's great, but I'm more worried about this rescue mission. The security here is pretty high tech."

"Is there any way we can get around it?"

"Not without hacking into the feed."

Crap! We looked dejectedly at each other as we realized our plan was slowly spiraling down the toilet. To be truthful, the first plan wasn't really thought out, and now we needed a new one.

Fortune smiled upon us in the form of a knock on our hotel door. Eddie peered through the peephole. "It's Murad," he whispered. "Should we let him in?"

"Just open the door a crack."

Eddie opened the door. "Yes?"

The same tall, thin man we had seen at the Sunny Side Up Retirement Home was kneeling before us as if we were going to knight him. "Your Majesty, it is so wonderful to meet you."

I smiled. Well, this turn of events could certainly work in our favor. "Why thank you! You may get up!" I told him.

He got up and smoothed back his long, green hair. "I would love for you and your Guardian to attend an exclusive dinner with me. I have so much to tell you about the new improvements."

"Of course, when is a good time?"

"In a few minutes?"

"Okay." *Someone's a little eager beaver*, I thought. "Give us a few minutes to get ready."

"I shall wait for you right here."

I quickly shut the door and pointed to my head, indicating to Eddie that we need to communicate telepathically. *It's like he wants us to find out that he's been abducting people*, I said. I unzipped the suitcase and pulled out our dress clothes: a three-piece black suit with a white dress shirt and a black tie for Eddie and a navy pantsuit with a white blouse for me. I began to get ready for dinner.

Eddie nodded as he got dressed. *He's incredibly over-self confident. We can use that to our advantage.*

Such as getting intel about the security system?

Yep.

"Okay, we're ready!" I said loudly. I opened up the door and found Murad standing off to the side. "Lead the way, Mr. Drum."

He beamed happily as if he were the teacher's pet. He led us out of the hallway and into an open archway leading into an equally ugly room about the size of a studio apartment. A half-dozen blackjack tables were scattered here and there. A few oblivious gamblers were seated at the brightly, sparkly slot machines. They must have forgotten that time exists outside the casino as they wear polyester jumpsuits in different shades of neon. They continuously inserted coins, pulled the lever hoping to hit the jackpot. "As Queen Rachel might have told you, the *Lucky Diamond* has been here for over twenty years," Murad told me.

"Wow!" I said feigning interest. "Has it always been a hotel and a casino?"

"Oh, yes. I have found that people love making deals and taking risks. It's the law of human nature."

"True."

"You must have one heck of a security system here," Eddie remarked.

Murad looked at the vampire curiously. "I had no idea Guardians were so interested in my security system."

Crap! I thought. *He's onto us.*

But my husband, ever the smooth talker, replied, "I just appreciate a security system that keeps a watchful eye on their guests' and employees' every move. I have suggested something similar to this to the queen."

Murad smiled eagerly. "Oh, then I highly suggest my system. It's impossible to hack into. Anyone who tries is sent over one thousand computer viruses."

"Interesting," Eddie said, but I knew what he was thinking. He was thinking of another way to get rid of the cameras.

Knowing my husband, it would be a more destructive way.

We came to a steel door at the back of the casino marked: Authorized Personnel Only. The only way to get in was through a high-tech panel. Murad bent down, and a laser beam scanned his eyes. Then he placed one of his hands flat on the screen. A series of complex lasers scanned it."Identify confirmed: A. Drum." A computer-generated voice boomed through the small area before the door unlocked and opened automatically.

Murad looked at Eddie with a smug grin. "This is the best part of my security system. Not only does it confirm identity through a retinal scan and fingerprints, but it also has a heat sensor. This is to prevent people from killing me or my associates and cutting off parts of their bodies. The system will know if someone is trying to break in or not."

"What happens if someone tries?" I asked.

Then for the first time, a truly evil smile crossed Murad's face. "If they try a retina scan with their eyes or the dismembered eye, their own eyes will be burned from their sockets with the lasers intensified a thousand times. The same with the fingerprint."

Eddie and I glanced at each other nervously. All right, scratch Plan B. Onto Plan C. "That's pretty harsh," I remarked.

"Your Majesty, you must control people with an iron fist or they will never learn," Murad replied as he led us down a bland passageway filled with only a few security cameras and no doors.

At the end of the passageway, he opened up a door into a large conference room with an oak table filled with food as if we had walked into this guy's Thanksgiving dinner. A twenty-pound turkey sat in the middle surrounded by a plate piled high with lobsters. There were five different kinds of pie, three different kinds of salads, a plate of caviar, steamed broccoli and cauliflower medley, brussel sprouts, and several plates with different kinds of meats. Murad had been expecting our arrival and was going all out for us. He pulled out a chair for me. "Have a seat, your Majesty."

My husband and I sat next to each other, and Murad sat directly across from me. Time for a little subtle interrogation. "So, Mr. Drum, how many employees do you have here?"

"In the casino and hotel itself, there are about twenty people."

"Wow, that seems like a small number for such a large establishment!"

Murad leaned forward as if he was about to tell me some deep dark secret. "The Lucky Diamond is only part of my property here."

"You have another business?"

"Queen Rachel never told you about the mines?"

"No," I replied. Jenny had mentioned the mines, but I wasn't going to tell him that.

"A long time ago, I discovered the true potential of this island. It is full of gems."

"That must turn a pretty profit."

Murad laughed. "It is if you don't tell your buyers that the gems aren't worth anything. In fact, let me show you something." He got up from the table and walked over to a small table against the wall. He opened one of the drawers and took out a remote control. He pointed it to a large flat-screen television and cued it up. "You'll get a kick out of this." We watched as the scene came to life.

Gunther was standing in front of the conference table, wincing in visible pain. He leaned against the table in a failing effort to support himself. Bone was sticking out of his left leg. He had his bow and arrow drawn and pointed at the disguised portal devil. The pain was battling against the satyr's determination to keep his weapon steady.

"I have no idea what you're talking about," Murad said.

"You knew that diamond you gave him was fake!" Gunther shouted angrily

Murad shrugged apathetically. "I'm not responsible for what happened once I gave that diamond to your friend."

"He's dead because of you!"

"It's not my fault your friend was too stupid to tell the difference between real and fake diamonds!"

Gunther lunged at Murad, but the portal devil pressed a hidden button under the table.

The door to the conference room quickly opened, and four bone creatures tackled the satyr. The bones in his left hip snapped apart loudly as one of the creatures hit him with a thick, metal club. He gave a bleat of pain as his legs buckled.

Murad, on the other hand, was laughing as if someone told him a hilarious joke. He paused the video. "You see, your Majesty, this man was stupid enough to try to kill me, and look where it got him."

I struggled to remain neutral as my anger bubbled up inside me. I wished I had my sword with me to enact justice. "What happened to him?" I asked.

Murad shrugged. "I had them take him to the incinerator." He shut off the television and put away the remote control. "Normally, I would have him healed with the Genesis fruit, but I'm having problems with rebellious workers lately."

"Oh," I said, pretending to nod in agreement. My heart was pounding in horror. I glanced down at the floor and noticed a small silver object lying near my feet. I dropped my napkin purposely on the floor. "Just one moment! Let me get my napkin!"

I bent down and scooped up the silver object along with my napkin. It was Gunther's lighter engraved with the message, "From E.B. With love." I realized this lighter must have been a gift from Enoch. Gunther would be heartbroken if he didn't get it back if he was still alive. I slipped the lighter into my pants pocket. The name Genesis triggered the memory of the dream I had about Dad and his friends. I needed to find out more. "What's a Genesis tree?"

"I found this fruit-bearing tree a long time ago. Each piece of fruit will temporarily heal injuries and will literally and permanently reverse your age by one year. A man in his fifties could eat several of them and be in his twenties again. And become immortal. The real magic is when you lay a dead body under the tree. It will bring someone back to life. Many of my workers have died in the mines, but I have brought most of them back to life. I have saved thousands of dollars and hours of paperwork using this method. It helps keep my workers' costs down significantly."

We heard a scuffle coming from behind the door and a loud crack. The door swung open and in walked two bone creatures dragging a semi-conscious Bruce Miller by the arms. Dark red blood ran down his face from a hidden head wound under his red hair. Apparently, he had eaten some of the Genesis fruit because he looked like he was in his late twenties. One of his green eyes was trying to focus on something.

"What now?" Murad asked one of the bone creatures in an irritated voice.

"He and the others were being insubordinate," the creature on the left replied.

"Again?" Murad turned to Eddie and I. "See what I have to put up with?" He said with a laugh.

Eddie quickly got up from his seat and walked over to Bruce. He placed one of his hands on the cook's shoulder. To my absolute shock, my husband suddenly punched the injured man once in the gut. Then without a word, he went back to his seat.

Murad saw the horrified look on my face. "You seem shocked by your Guardian's actions."

"Yes," I stammered, "I wasn't expecting him to do that. Could you leave us as I obviously need to discipline him?" Murad laughed. "Of course, I shall return once I take care of my little problem in the mines." Everyone left the conference room, leaving me to stare at my husband in shock. I wasn't sure if there were any listening devices in the room so I decided to speak to Eddie telepathically. *I know you don't like Bruce, but come on! The guy's injured.*

Don't worry, Shell! I didn't hurt him.

Yeah, you did! You punched him in the gut.

No, it only looked like I did. I threw a fake punch so that I could place a tracker on him. Eddie saw the perplexed look on my face. *I got some trackers from the armory. They not only will give us a constant location, but it will also monitor his heartbeat and pulse.*

Geesh, Eddie, why didn't you tell me this earlier?

Because your reaction needed to be genuine so Murad wouldn't get suspicious.

The door handle began to turn as we heard voices. *Quick, yell at me or something!* Eddie told me subliminally as he quickly dropped to one knee and hung his head in false shame.

The door opened, and Murad popped his head in. "And another thing!" I pretended to shout at Eddie. "You do not think for yourself! You are here to do my bidding! Do I make myself clear?"

Eddie made a pretty convincing solemn face. "Yes, your Majesty. It won't happen again."

"It better not," I replied, securing the deal with my angry queen act. "Mr. Drum, I am very tired, and this unsightly interaction with my Guardian has made me too upset to eat!" I threw up my hands in exaggerated frustration.

"I understand, your Majesty," Murad said. "I shall have you escorted back to your room."

"Thank you!" I nudged Eddie with my foot. "Come along, Guardian!"

Drama queen much? My long-suffering husband asked me.

This was your idea. I managed to hide my smile as Murad

made a phone call to have us taken back to our room.

Two creepy mannequins took us back to our room in uncomfortable silence. Seriously, being around living mannequins can kill any fun vibe. Eddie quickly searched the room for listening devices, and once he declared it safe, we sat on the edge of the bed. The hidden anger within me exploded. "He sent Gunther to his death! And what if Murad did the same thing to Dad and Amelia." Tears began to well up in my eyes. Eddie put his arm around me and pulled me close to him. "It'll be okay, babe."

I wiped away the tears with the back of my hand as I leaned against him. "Did you have a vision or something?" I asked.

Eddie smiled as he kissed the top of my head. "Of course not. I just don't want you to give up. We've come so far, and whatever happens, we'll work through it together."

This was one of the many reasons I fell in love with my husband. His kindness and undying love for me. We crawled under the covers of the hotel room, and I snuggled next to my Guardian. "I know. I'm just worried." I decided to change the subject. "Will you report what we've learned back to the *Monte Carlo*? I wasn't kidding about being tired." I was also emotionally drained. I laid my head on Eddie's chest, listening to his slow, steady heartbeat.

"Of course," he said. After putting one arm around me, he pressed his comlink with his free hand. "Monte Carlo, are you there?"

"I can barely hear you, sire," came Cassius' voice through both our comlinks.

"All right," Eddie said as he absentmindedly stroked my hair. "I'll make it quick. We have a lead here. At least, one of my father-in-law's friends is down here. We just don't exactly know where they are. Shelly and I are going to search the hotel when it gets quiet in a few more hours."

"All right. Thanks for the update, sire. Stay safe."

"We will, Cassius. Signing off." Eddie turned off the comlink and kissed me. "I think I'll put a ward spell on our room."

"Good idea," I said, not moving from my comfy position on his chest. "Murad seems like the kind of guy who'd kill us in our sleep." I barely heard my husband utter the magic words as I fell into a dreamless sleep.

Chapter Ten:
"Authorized Personnel Only" Means Nothing to Us

"Shell, wake up." Eddie gently shook my shoulder. I opened my eyes to see my husband out of bed. With magic, he had shrunk our weapons suitcase down to the size of a cell phone and was slipping it into his pants pocket.

I threw off the covers and rubbed my eyes as I gave myself a few moments to wake up. My backpack was sitting on the suite's green pull-out couch, and I noticed that Eddie had already retrieved Vengeance and his utility belt from it. I got out of bed and walked over to the backpack. I pulled out my utility belt with my unique assortment of weapons already on it. As soon as I clipped it on my pants' belt loops, I pulled out my favorite weapon: an old book. I said the incantation written on the red cover, "Knowledge is Power." Green sparkles swirled around the book as it began to morph into my deadly sheathed sword. I slung Knowledge onto my back and adjusted the strap across my chest. "Honey, where are the first aid kits?"

Eddie reached into his pocket and pulled out two tiny first aid kits the size of a deck of playing cards. "Here they are," he said as he handed them to me.

I slipped them into my pocket. "You ready?"

Eddie took out his cell phone and activated the tracker before handing the phone to me. "I am. I'll get us there as safely as possible if you want to be in charge of the tracker."

"No problem."

He unlocked the door and peered out in the hallway. "All clear."

I looked at the tracker. "We have to turn right, and it looks like Bruce is still alive." We nonchalantly walked down the hall like a couple exploring the hotel at a cosplay convention, not at all like two people looking for abductees. I further perpetuated the illusion by taking Eddie's hand. I realized we were taking the same path Murad had led us down earlier.

What made our journey even weirder was the lack of hotel guests. Even the casino was completely empty. I pointed out this unnerving little fact to Eddie.

"That's not at all creepy. Maybe everyone's asleep?"

"Or we could be the only real guests here. Did you get a good look at the people sitting at the slot machines?"

Eddie looked at me thoughtfully. "Not really. Now that you mention it, I didn't even hear heartbeats."

I nodded in agreement. "The living mannequins must be posing as guests and employees of the hotel and casino. What happened to all the other guests?"

"Murad might have kidnapped them and forced them to work in the mines. It sounds like your sister knew about this whole enterprise and agreed with it."

"We are in a literal Hotel California."

We came to a stop when we got to the door marked: Authorized Personnel Only. The only other room in the surprisingly non-secured hallway was an opened broom closet. I mean, shouldn't every villain have some form of security cameras outside the entrance to his secret lair? Come on, people! This is villainy 101. Then I remembered the door's unusual quirks. There was no way we could get in without immediate death. We're both pretty attached to our eyeballs and hands. "Now what?" I asked.

Eddie eyed the chemicals in the closet. Even without reading his mind, I knew he was calculating the best concoction for maximum explosion. "What about some form of wanton destruction?" he suggested.

"And alert Murad? Because nothing says 'intruder' like a huge explosion."

"I'm just spitballing ideas here. You're the brains of this operation."

I rubbed the bridge of my nose with two of my fingers. "I know. Just let me think. What's a possible way for us to get in safely?"

Eddie heard the footsteps before I did. He tapped my shoulder and pointed up. We jumped and stuck to the ceiling like spiders. We waited breathlessly as the people got closer. It turned out to be James Mallory and Gregory Madison.

"Did you hear him last time?" Mallory said with a cruel laugh.

Eddie and I watched him stare into the retina scan. My heart pounded in sheer terror. We were right above them, and they had no idea. One false move and we would need to be rescued.

"I never thought I would enjoy beating the crap out of Anderson, but it keeps getting better and better," said Madison.

"Especially when he or his buddies try to play the heroes." Mallory scanned his palm.

"Some people never change."

The door identified the men on the ground and swung open. We saw our only chance. Quiet as spiders, Eddie and I followed Madison and Mallory into the next room. We found ourselves in a small cavern with a tunnel entrance only a few feet away. We waited until the men entered the darkened tunnel and were out of sight before dropping to the floor without a sound.

"That went well," Eddie said.

"Yeah, good thing they didn't look up, or we'd be goners,"

I said. I retrieved his cell phone from my pocket and checked the tracker. "At least, we're heading in the right direction. Let's go."

We started walking into the dim passage. There was barely any light, but I didn't want to waste my husband's cell phone battery if I turned on the flashlight app. "Do you have a flashlight in that Batman belt of yours?"

"I don't think we should use a flashlight. It could attract unwanted attention."

"All right, galavanting in the dark, it is," I said as I took another step. Immediately, a light flickered above our heads, giving a clear path of a couple of yards ahead. "Well, someone heard my sarcastic plea."

"Sure," Eddie said with a roll of his eyes. As we started to walk out of the light's reach, we were cast into darkness again. Only for a step or two. Another light flooded the darkness. "Not a miracle, but I'm guessing motion detector lights."

"I guess it saves on electricity. Every villain's dream: low electric bills."

This went on for a while. One minute, it was dark, and then it was light again. The whole experience lost its novelty after the second time which really irritated me. "What's the purpose of this lighting system?" I complained to my husband. "It's so stupid. You're only creating potential workplace lawsuits by installing motion detector lights in a completely dark, underground tunnel."

"I think the purpose is just to irritate you."

I was about to reply with an equally smart remark when my vampiric hearing heard familiar voices coming from somewhere deeper into the dark. "Amelia?" I dropped Eddie's cell phone and took off running.

I barely heard the vampire call after me as I concentrated on following my stepmother's voice. It was as if something was guiding me to her. Black and gold sparkles filled my vision as I ran even faster, and I didn't even feel my body change. I dropped to all four, powerful legs as my black panther body easily navigated the narrow passages, increasing my speed.

My vision had narrowed into a binocular view with the eyes of a big cat. Somewhere in my journey, the lights above me had changed from motion detectors to regular floodlights. I veered off to the left. A panther scream escaped my mouth as I leaped at the man holding the gun.

He let out a scream of agonizing horror as my teeth bit down on his arm. As I yanked down, I heard the bones of his arm cracking under the pressure of my jaws. The gun flew out of his hand and skittered away. I released him and quickly put myself between him and his victim. "What the—?" Madison bellowed as he cradled his broken arm and stared at me in stunned horror.

In my haste, I hadn't properly assessed the situation. I had lept in a small open room that served as the entrance to what looked like some kind of an execution room. Dried blood splatter patterned the walls.

I glanced at the woman I was protecting. The heaviness I had been harboring in my heart ever since I learned my parents were missing was lifted. It was my stepmother.

I turned and snarled at Madison as I deliberately put myself between Amelia and him. He could try to make a run for the gun, but he would never make it with me in the room.

Madison foolishly attempted to run, but it was cut short when the butt of a long, golden war scythe hit him in the back of the head. He stumbled forward and fell to the ground with a thump, kicking up dust as he went down.

"You okay, babe?" Eddie asked me as he poked the unconscious body with Vengeance.

I changed back to my regular old self. "Yeah. You?"

"I'm good." He seemed to be out of breath. "Holy crap! You're fast!" He pulled out a handful of zip ties and secured the unconscious man's hands and feet.

As soon as I cut away her bonds, I reached down and helped my stepmother to her feet. "You hurt?" I asked her.

Amelia wrapped her arms around me and breathed a huge sigh of relief. "I'm just so glad you and Eddie are all right."

I brushed back the tears of happiness from my eyes. There would be time for a more joyful reunion once everyone was safe and sound. I inspect the metal collar around Amelia's neck. "Any idea how to take this off?"

She shook her head full of black hair. It was then that I noticed how young she looked, around my age. She must have been eating the Genesis fruit during her captivity. "Your father and his friends have tried various ways when our captors weren't looking."

"Dad's okay?"

"He's fine. He's been so worried about you and Robin."

"Robin and Roger are aboard the *Monte Carlo*. The girls and Dirk are back in Peregrin," Eddie said as he came over. He gave his stepmother-in-law a tight hug. He looked at the collar. "I've got an idea. I think Shelly and I can pull it apart with our combined vampire strength."

Amelia nodded. "Give it a try."

Eddie and I each took one side of the collar, and all three of us did a count of three. Then my husband and I slowly pulled the metal collar apart. We were careful not to cut Amelia on the sharp edges.

As soon as she was free, a huge smile came across her face. She flexed her fingers, no doubt feeling the tingle of her magical ability coming back to her. "That feels good. Come on. I'll take you to the others."

We followed her through the passageway on the other side. I asked her about the blood splatters in the room we had just left. "That is Murad's execution room. Reserved especially for what he calls 'troublemakers.'" She shook her head in disgust.

I didn't need to ask anything more, and I changed the subject. "We have two first aid kits, but I don't know who's injured or not."

"Fortunately, we only have two major injuries. Gunther's injuries are pretty severe, but it's Bruce's injuries I'm most worried about. He has a major concussion that will heal with at least five unicorn pills."

Eddie and I froze in our tracks. "Gunther's alive?" I asked. "I thought Murad had him sent to the incinerator. At least that's what he told us."

"Dusty saved his life, but I think Gunther's left hip is shattered, and his left leg is broken in two places," Amelia replied. "How did you find us?"

I told her everything that had transpired in the past week. "Murad thinks I'm like Rachel, which I am not."

Amelia said nothing. She definitely remembered the last time I saw her and Dad, and that was a sore spot.
I hated this hidden unease between us. I stepped in front of her and blocked her path. "I forgive you," I blurted out.

"Shelly, you have every right—,"she started to say.

"Let me talk, please. I now know that you were trying to protect me from Rachel's rage. I forgive you, and I'm so sorry for causing this rift between us." I threw my arms around her as I fought back the tears. "I've already lost my mom, and I don't want to lose you."

"It's all right, sweetheart. I accept your forgiveness."

"Let's find everyone else and get out of here," I said.

We all headed into a brightly lit cavern with about ten closed doors leading to other places. An elfin woman I recognized as Libby Miller was kneeling on the ground, cradling her semi-conscious husband, Bruce. Tears pooled in her purple eyes as her long blond hair fell across her face. A bloodied bandage was wrapped around Bruce's head. It was the scene at one of the long tables that hit me hard. My father was sitting on one of the tree stumps that served as crude chairs. His head was cupped in his hands, and he was crying softly. Another man and another woman were sitting on either side of him, comforting him.

"Timothy!" Amelia rushed forward and threw her arms

around my father. "It's alright! I'm okay!"

Dad looked up. "Oh, my god, Amelia! I thought I had lost you!" He kissed her passionately as they tightly embraced each other. Tears of joy ran down both of their faces. He finally noticed the missing collar. "What happened?"

Eddie and I stepped forward. "Hi, Dad!" I said.

Dad let go of his wife and gave me a huge bear hug. Then he did the same thing to my husband. "What are you doing here?" He asked me once he let go of us.

"We came to rescue you," I said. "First things first, introductions." I pointed to Eddie. "Eddie, that's Andrew and Natalie Baker," I said to the stunned couple who was comforting my father.

"Andrew, Natalie, this is my husband, Eddie Van Helsing." Andrew looked at my father in shock. "Who is this woman?" He asked him.

"It's me, Shelly. Timothy's daughter."

"You're supposed to be dead because that's what Timothy and Amelia have been telling everyone since they got here."

"Does undead count?" I asked.

Dad broke in. "I lied to protect both Shelly and Robin."

Bruce attempted to sit up. "Libby and I did the same thing." He tried to focus, but I could tell he needed medical attention fast.

"Let's get you some unicorn pills," I said as I took the two first aid kits out of my pockets. I placed them on the table.

Eddie waved his hand over them and said, "Maximum five." The tiny kits grew to their normal size.

I popped open the latch on the first one and looked for the bottle of unicorn pills. When I found it, I discovered we had a problem. The bottle only contained six pills.

Amelia and Natalie were going through the other kit when I showed them. I knew by their disappointed faces that I had the only bottle. My stepmother frowned. "It's barely enough. Bruce will need at least five of them to heal."

Natalie looked at the pills. "What are these?"

"Pills made from unicorn horns," Amelia explained. "The magic inside them will heal anything."

"Similar to the Genesis fruit then?"

"Yes, but the pills don't permanently reverse your age and

make you immortal."

"What about Gunther?" I asked Amelia. "You said he's severely injured."

"That's the thing. One pill might help with the pain, but he needs surgery."

I knew what I had to do. "You're the medical expert, Amelia."

She nodded and divided the pills: five for Bruce and one for Gunther. She knew how concerned I was for the satyr. "He has been eating some of the fruit which has helped a little."

"Okay, but I think we need to get him the medication as soon as possible."

Dad nodded. "We'll give Bruce the medicine he needs. You and Eddie go see your friend. He's in Dusty's room which is the very last door on the left."

My husband and I went to the steel door Dad had told us about. I knocked on it. I heard a vaguely familiar voice telling us to come in. I turned the knob and went inside.

The layout of the room was shockingly decent. If one didn't know better, you'd think that we had just entered a very basic hotel room minus the television. A simple bathroom was off to the right side of one of the two full-size beds. Sitting upright on one of them was our private secretary next to another man. The now young-looking satyr was holding the man's hand and smiling as they talked.

Their conversation abruptly ended the moment we entered the room. "Your majesties?" Gunther said as he immediately let go of the man's hand. He tried to move and put some space between himself and the dirty-blonde haired man, but he winced in pain.

I took the unicorn pill out of my pocket and handed it to the satyr. "I have something that'll help with the pain."

He looked at me with uncertainty before taking the pill. He popped it in his mouth and swallowed it dry.

The man he was with looked intently at me before saying. "You look very familiar. Do I know you?"

That's when I recognized him, it was Natalie's brother, Dusty. "Dusty, it's me, Shelly."

"Shelly Anderson?"

I had not seen Dusty Williams in several years, but he

looked to be in his late twenties, not late fifties. "It's Shelly Van Helsing, now," I said. Every adult down here must have been eating the Genesis fruit.

"Okay." He looked at Gunther. "Is she your boss?"

The satyr nodded. A look of pure terror briefly crossed his face, but he quickly masked it with a smile. "Yes, Queen Shelly and King Eddie rule Peregrin. What are you doing here?"

"A rescue mission. First things, let's get that collar off you, Dusty."

"It wouldn't come off. I've tried," the former police detective said.

"That's because you didn't have two vampires to help you," I said with a grin. Eddie and I took the collar in both our hands and slowly pulled it apart. I glanced over at Gunther who looked terrified at what we were doing. I desperately wanted to tell him that Eddie and I knew about him being gay, and we're okay with it. Then I remembered my promise to Cassius. Just treat him as you've always treated him, I told myself.

"How do you feel?" Eddie asked Dusty.

The man rubbed his neck. "Great!" He looked over at

Gunther. "How are you feeling?"

"A little better," the satyr said.

I looked at the makeshift splint on Gunther's left leg. Even with my lack of medical knowledge, I knew it would be detrimental to his health if we tried to move him. I pressed the comlink. "Queen to the *Monte Carlo*, come in, please."

The airship's captain crackled in my ear. "This is Captain Cassius, your Majesty. What is your status?"

"Everyone is here, including Gunther, but he's been injured pretty badly. His left leg and hip are broken. My stepmother thinks he'll need emergency surgery. Is there any way you can send the teleportation spheres to my location?"

I heard noises in the background before Cassius answered. "We can barely pinpoint your location."

I wondered if the combination of being underground and the mining facilities were interfering with the airship's radar system. "Can you send the spheres?"

"Only two, and only for a minute or so."

I looked at Gunther and Dusty. The satyr definitely liked my old friend. "Do it." A few moments later, two floating orbs appeared between the four of us. They hovered in the air, flicking in and out of focus. Gunther immediately placed both of his hands on one of them. "Dusty, place both your hands on the other one," I told him. "They will teleport both of you up the Monte Carlo. Delilah will have a medical team on standby when you and Gunther get there."

Dusty never hesitated. He linked one of his arms with the satyr's arm and took the sphere with both hands. "Ready," he said.

Eddie pressed his comlink. "Cassius, this is the king. We're all set. Gunther and his friend, Dusty, are coming up."

Eddie and I had never watched someone use the spheres. We had always been on the receiving end. The orbs glowing brightly for a few seconds as the men's bodies faded into sparkling golden lights. Then they vanished altogether. I looked at my husband. "You think Cassius might be a Star Trek fan?"

"No doubt."

Cassius's voice appeared in my ear. "Gunther and his friend are safely on board, and Delilah has taken Gunther to the infirmary. I wish we could send more spheres, but we keep losing your exact location.”

“Not a problem. We can handle it from here. I’m glad to know they are both safe.” I ended the conversation with a single tap to the comlink.” I glanced at Eddie. “All right, this changes my plan significantly.”

Eddie raised an eyebrow at me. “You had actually had a plan this time?”

“More like the bare remnants of one. My plan was to find everyone and have Cassius teleport us out of here.”

Eddie shrugged. “It’s more than what we normally have.”

“You should know by now just how many of my plans I come up with on the spot.”

“We are living on the edge.”

I headed out of the door to go back to the main living area. I wondered how Bruce’s head was doing, but more worried about how we were going to get everyone out.

Everyone listened politely as I told them what had happened in Dusty’s room. “I get why you sent Dusty and

Gunther on ahead, but you do realize that was really stupid," Bruce said. Apparently, he was feeling back to his old, obnoxious self again.

I could sense the tension in Eddie's body as he readied himself to defend my honor. It was much appreciated, but not necessary. "Hey, don't bite the hand that just saved your life." I looked at everyone. "Okay, what's the best way out of here?"

Dad looked at Eddie and me incredulously. "The only way out of here is death. Believe me, we've tried."

"But did you have weapons?" I asked.

Andrew raised a skeptical eyebrow. "What weapons?"

Eddie took the miniaturized luggage out of his pants pocket. He said the magic words, and the suitcase grew to its normal size. He unzipped the bag and showed the array of weapons. "Take your pick!" Eddie said.

Dad, Andrew, and Bruce looked inside and picked their weapons. Still having law enforcement in their blood, they all picked various kinds of guns. Libby refused to take a weapon. Natalie chose a small dagger, but Amelia's pick surprised me the most. She chose two steel, circular chakras.

"You know how to use these?" I asked her.

"I may be a bit rusty, but I do remember my training from when I was a child."

I heard slow clapping behind us and I turned around.

"Did you think that you could just walk on in here and disrupt my workforce, your Majesty?" Murad asked. I noticed his visage was flickering in and out as if he was struggling to maintain his humanoid disguise.

I was done with his nonsense. "This is wrong, Murad!" I said. "Let these people go!"

His disguise melted away instantly as every facade vanished. His true self took me by surprise. He still had on the ridiculously expensive suit, but under it, we could all see his red skin gleaming like wet blood. His soulless eyes on his flaming, black skull seemed to bore into the very depths of my soul. Even the thousands of tiny green snakes on his head stared at me, watching for any sign of defeat.

I swallowed my shock and drew Knowledge from her sheath as I took a fighting stance. "By order of Queen Michelle, ruler of all Peregrin, I hereby command you to let these people go!" I kept my voice steady as a somewhat shaky restaurant table.

His reaction was not what I was expecting. "I answer to no one!" His bellow was so loud it literally blew me across the room, nearly slamming me into the wall. "I'm the most powerful being in here. You shall answer to me!" He began to stalk towards me.

Eddie was the first to go down. He didn't have time to activate any of his spells before Murad's magic flung him across the room. He did have the sense to curl up in a ball before slamming against the wall next to me.

Murad grabbed my father by the neck and started to cut off his air supply. Dad hadn't fully recovered his magical ability to stretch himself yet and struggled in vain to breathe.

"Stop!" I screamed at Murad. I couldn't bear the thought of watching my father die when I had come so close to rescuing him. The next few words burst from my mouth in a moment of frantic desperation. "I'll make a deal with you!"

The portal devil loosen his death grip on Dad's throat only a tiny bit as he looked at me in bewildered amusement. No one was stupid enough to make deals with a devil. No one that is, except for me. "I'm intrigued. Go on."

My mind began to haphazardly put together a not-too-well thought out plan. "Let my Guardian and I fight your manticore in the arena. If we defeat him, you have to let everyone here go."

"And if you don't?"

Eddie and I would most likely be dead if we lost, but at the moment, I tried to think of happier thoughts. "If we lose, then I will serve you here."

"And your Guardian as well."

I glanced over at Eddie who nodded grimly. "Yes."

An angelic smile laced with malevolence crossed the portal devil's face. "I agree to your terms. Normally, you would battle weaponless, but since I admire your tenacity. You and your Guardian may only use one weapon, and no magic."

"Agreed." I had just sealed our death sentence.

Murad dropped Dad to the ground like a discarded rag. He snapped his fingers. Inky black smoke filled the room. When it cleared, the only people left were Eddie, the portal devil, and me. Every single weapon Dad, Amelia, and their friends had gathered from the suitcase lay in a crumpled, tangled pile on the dirt floor. The only weapons that weren't twisted or bent to the point of uselessness were Knowledge and Vengeance. Both the sword and war scythe were impervious to magic and hadn't been touched

My eyes filled with panic. What had Murad done? "Where are they?" I demanded.

"I am giving you and your Guardian a few minutes alone to prepare for your ultimate defeat. I have sent the others to the arena. They will be witnesses." He snapped his fingers again and vanished in another cloud of smoke.

I picked up my sword with my shaking hands as I considered what I had just done. I wasn't even sure that this plan was going to succeed. Now my father and stepmother would be forced to watch their daughter and son-in-law get torn to shreds by a manticore.

The vampire got up relatively unharmed from the magic attack and retrieved his war scythe. "You okay, Shell?" He asked.

I looked at him. "I don't think my plan will work this time." My voice was barely above a whisper.

Eddie was about to say my plans always work, but he saw

the worried look on my face. He sat down next to me. "What makes you think it won't?"

"I've never been up against someone as powerful as Murad. I don't know if we will even survive fighting his manticore. I just don't want Dad and Amelia to watch us get torn apart due to my stupidity."

He put an arm around me and pulled me close to him. "Everything will be alright, Shell. We'll get through this. We always do."

I managed a smile as I leaned against him. His unwavering trust in my crazy plans never ceases to amaze me. I kissed him briefly. "Thank you for making me feel better."

He smiled. "You're welcome. We've got this, Shell. I mean, we're talking about manticores. How hard will it be?"

Chapter Eleven:
Manticores in Mirrors are Bigger than They Appear

When Murad whisked us away to his giant death arena, we found ourselves unnerved. The arena looked like Murad had ripped from the pages of Roman history. My husband and I found ourselves standing in a dusty area the same size as a soccer field. The 50-foot cement walls surrounding us were stained with blood.

I glanced up into the circular seating around us and spotted Dad and Amelia looking really nervously down at us. Andrew and Natalie were next to them, both of them had a hand on their daughter's shoulder. Bruce was holding his breath as he held his wife's hand. The collars hadn't been replaced. I had a sinking feeling that Murad would replace them as soon as Eddie and I were defeated. He probably wanted to give his prisoners a false sense of hope.

In an outlandishly decorated box-office seat that matched the decor of the casino was the smug portal devil. Flanking him was Mallory on his right side and Madison and Kramer on his right. Murad sat up and addressed the spectators. "Ladies and gentlemen," he said, "you are about to witness the death of your queen and her Guardian. Let this be a lesson to all of you: No one ever leaves here alive."

Eddie looked at me. "He doesn't know us very well, does he?"

I managed a smile. I was preoccupied with the steel door lining the wall. Why was it 50-feet high? "Just how big are manticores?"

The vampire shrugged. "I don't know. Never seen one before."

I slowly pressed my back against his as I readied myself for anything and everything. Someone large and heavy rammed against the steel door. I could see the outside hinges strain against the blows.

Deafening roars echoed throughout the stadium. Then the door directly in front of me opened. Let me preface that Eddie and I grossly overestimated our knowledge of this creature. "Holy crap!" I whispered in shock. "That thing is huge!" Huge as in T-Rex huge. The lion-like creature towered over us by a good 20-feet. The body was only half its length, but the powerful scorpion tail was much longer. Murad had been especially cruel to it by strapping down its huge, leather wings tight against its body with an electrical rope. Not being able to fly and no doubt very hungry made him quite dangerous. Oh, we were so dead.

"Shield!" Eddie yelled to me.

I quickly pressed the button on the underside of my bracelet. Truth popped up and prevented the huge stinger from impaling me. I swung my sword at the manticore and was horrified to discover the fur was like a steel coat of armor. "We've got a problem," I told Eddie.

"I can clearly see that." His war scythe had done no better. "How are we supposed to stop this thing?"

I glanced at him. "I thought you knew," I said, dodging

another deadly swipe from the stinger.

"Me? What makes you think I know anything about manticores?"

"Because you said-and I quote-'we're talking manticores. How hard can they be?'"

"I just assumed you were going to pull out one of your random bits of trivia from your butt and save our lives." He quickly took several steps back to avoid getting stung.

"I think we need to work on our communication the next time we do something as crazy as this." I backed up with him as my brain frantically attempted to recall any knowledge of manticores I had absorbed in my life which was absolutely nothing. I glanced at the creature. Okay, it looks like a lion. Then I remembered an article I had read ages ago on how to survive a mountain lion attack. A desperate idea slowly formed. "Do what I do," I told Eddie. I puffed out my chest and made myself as big as possible, and then I began to bang the hilt of my sword against my shield.

Eddie looked at me as if I had gone completely crazy as he followed my lead.

Our noise definitely did not scare the manticore. It snarled at us and began to run. My brain went into deep panic mode as it searched for any usable idea. *Manticores are essentially big cats, right? Eddie, use Alonzo's favorite app!* I mentally told the vampire.

It took him a few seconds to realize what I was saying. He dropped Vengeance and took his cell phone out of his pocket. He pointed the phone at the manticore. He glanced up at my father who was clearly confused by the vampire's actions.

The creature stopped in its tracks the second it saw the red dot and pounced at it. Then it let out a painful yowl as a powerful surge of electricity ran through the rope around its body. It jumped several feet in the air. The second it landed on the ground, it was whimpering in pain.

I glanced up at Murad and noticed a small, round object in his palm. He was torturing the manticore. "Get up, you lousy beast!" The portal devil yelled at the manticore.

Anger bubbled up in me like boiling oil. *We need to get that rope off him*, I mentally told my husband.

What? Why?

Because Murad is hurting Blinky and forcing him to attack us.

Who is Blinky?

Fred and Paula's pet manticore. Marcie told us about him, remember?

Oh, yeah.

Another crazy plan began to form in my mind. *Keep Blinky busy with that laser pointer.* Once Eddie began to distract the manticore, I circled around to the creature's side. I took several steps back before breaking into a run and launched myself onto Blinky's back.

"Shelly!" My stepmom yelled. "Watch out for the stinger!"

I scrambled out of the way of the giant tail. I slid Knowledge under one of the ropes and pulled up. I should've been keeping a closer eye on Murad. Just as my sword was cutting through the last strand, an electrical surge ran up my sword and through my body. I toppled off Blinky and fell to the ground. I lay there like a slug. The wind knocked out of me. I saw the manticore spread its wings and immediately fly out of the arena. *Be free, Blinky,* I thought to myself. *You deserve it.*

"Kill them!" Murad shouted at someone. He definitely was getting the sore loser award.

Eddie was crouching by my side in an instant. "You okay?"

The only thing I could lift was an eyebrow. "I just got electrocuted, honey. How do you think I feel?"

Eddie jammed Vengeance upright in the sand to free up his hands. "Now would be the time to get up if you can."

"Give me a minute or two," I said.

He nodded without looking at me. "Duracell!" A little blue ball of energy appeared between his palms. He expanded it until it was the size of a basketball and then threw it at the black and red blur speeding toward us.

The energy ball hit Kramer in the legs. The cruel man stumbled and crashed head-first into the wall. He lay there unconscious and barely breathing as blood pooled around his head. It was hard to come up with sympathy for someone who had kidnapped my parents.

"Kill them!" The portal demon screamed at Mallory and Madison.

"No way!" Madison protested. "You saw what that vampire did to Kramer!"

"He knew the consequences," Murad replied. "Do it, or I will kill you."

"You promised us riches and power, not fighting vampires," Madison said. Obviously, Eddie's magic had scared him.

Murad angrily grabbed Madison by the collar of his expensive shirt and tossed the former detective into the arena. He would have hit the ground hard if he didn't turn himself in a liquid form. Really gross. Once he morphed back to his normal, evil self, he pulled a whip off his belt and snapped it at us. I had fully recovered and took my place by my husband's side, our weapons ready. Eddie and I looked at each other and shook our heads. This moron really thought he would defeat us with a whip. I caught the whip in my shield hand and yanked hard. The re-cracking of his arm was so satisfying.

Once he was within reach, Eddie quickly coldcocked him and down went the unconscious Madison. "Two down, and two to go," Eddie said to me. He looked up at the stands and smiled.

"Looks like they got their powers back."

I followed his gaze. Remains of the bone creatures were scattered everywhere. Dad, Bruce, and Andrew had overpowered and were now armed. Mallory tried to stop them, but Dad hit him hard in the solar plexus. All three lackeys of the portal devil were down for the count.

Murad snapped his fingers and vanished in a puff of smoke. He reappeared directly in front of us. He shoved Eddie aside as if the vampire were a piece of paper and grabbed me by the throat. "How dare you defy me?"

I struggled to speak, but no words could come from me. I dropped my sword and tried to pry his hands off me, but it was like trying to move a mountain. Time slowed down as the devil lifted me off the ground and squeezed harder. You can't kill a vampire simply by choking her, but you could still break her neck and crush her vertebrae. I started to blackout as my brain fought for oxygen.

Then I heard a whoosh as a blade cut through bone and muscle. I could smell the coppery scent of blood as it splattered against my face. The flames on Murad's skull head extinguished as it was disconnected from his body. The death grip was released as both the portal devil's body and myself crumpled to the ground. I looked up expecting to see Eddie. Instead, my father reached out his hand to me.

"It's all right, Shelly. He's gone," Dad said.

I threw my arms around my father and hugged him. "Thank you, Dad," I rasped.

He set the bloodied battle-ax down. "You're welcome. No one hurts my daughter."

"Shell, are you okay?" Eddie asked as he ran up to me.

I let go of my father and nearly fell into my husband's arms as I felt my legs turn to jelly. Murad's death grip had taken a lot out of me. "I'm okay. Let's get everyone out of here."

Chapter Twelve:

Healing the Past, Changing the Future

It took a couple of hours for the crew of the Monte Carlo to safely transport every prisoner back to the airship. Delilah was still performing surgery on Gunther's leg and hip, and so my stepmother and Natalie took control of the situation and began to tend to anyone's medical needs. Once everyone was safe and accounted for, I instructed Cassius to take us home to Peregrin.

While Eddie went to help the bridge crew, I found Dad sitting by himself in the galley. The smell of Leo's garlic Mac and Cheese filled the room. The minotaur was handing him a plate of the delicious meal and was saying, "This is Queen Shelly and King Eddie's favorite meal on the ship."

Dad took one bite of it and nodded in agreement. "This is really good."

Leo smiled. "It's an old family recipe." He turned around to see me standing behind him. "Hello, your Majesty! Would you like some food?"

"If it's not too much trouble, Leo," I said. Once the cook left, I pointed to the seat across from Dad. "Is this seat taken?"

Dad sipped the delicious smelling mint coffee as he shook his head. There was an awkward silence as I sat down until he finally spoke. "How's your sister?"

"Evil and bat guano crazy."

Dad smiled sadly. "So she hasn't changed one bit."

"Hatred will do that to a person. She told me that you refused to let her come to Mom's funeral."

Dad nodded. "I thought I was protecting you from her. Amelia had pleaded with me to let her come, but I didn't listen to her. I should've let Rachel come to grieve for Mom." Dad sighed. "That's why your sister is so angry with me, isn't it?"

"I think it contributed to it," I said without judgment.

Dad cursed softly, a rare thing. "I wish I could go back in

time to change things.”

I thought about the law I was about to change. “Dad,” I said, “I don’t know of any kind of time machine out there, but I can tell you one thing.”

“What’s that?”

“You can’t change the past, but you can definitely change the future.” I swallowed hard. “By accepting my forgiveness. I shouldn’t have yelled at you and Amelia that night. Can you ever forgive me for being such a jerk?”

“Of course, Shelly!” Dad got up from his seat and came around the table. I got from my seat because I knew what was coming next. We both embraced. “Your sister might not ever forgive me, but will you?”

“Of course.”

We hugged for a little more before we were interrupted by Leo with the food. We broke apart and sat back down. I began to eat my food.

“You did a good thing,” Dad said.

“What?”

“Rescuing us. Putting your own life ahead of everyone

else. Mom would be so proud of you, as I am."

I blushed. "Thanks, Dad." Then I asked the question that had been bothering me ever since I discovered them missing. "How did you get involved with Murad?"

"It all started with Matt's disappearance. I suspected something from this world was involved, but didn't tell anyone. Because who would believe me? Do you remember the drug raid that got me fired? I saw Murad conversing with Mallory right before he opened a portal. When we got to Zephyr, I began to investigate other disappearances similar to Matt's."

"Did Amelia know what you were doing?" I asked. I couldn't even imagine my stepmom being onboard with Dad doing police work on the side.

"Not until Murad kidnapped us. She's already reamed me out for that." He smiled. "Anyway, Andrew and his family were already there, as was Dusty when we were brought to the mines. Andrew and Dusty had been given an anonymous tip about Matt's whereabouts. Mallory got wind that they were getting a little too close to the truth and had them kidnapped as well."

"An anonymous tip?"

"Yeah, Andrew said a woman with black, sparkling hair had come into the station and said Matt was still alive and was a slave laborer."

I looked at my father in surprise. "Was her name Colleen?"

"Yes, how did you know?"

I told him about the mystery woman who had shown up in my office last week. He looked puzzled. "I'm pretty sure Andrew said she was human, not a minotaur."

"When Marcie encountered her, she was a Winged One." "I would say she is a shape-shifter, but I've never heard of one not showing up on cameras."

I was about to say something when I looked up to see Dusty coming to our table. The satyr must have been out of surgery, "How's Gunther?"

"Much better," Dusty replied as he sat down. "He's resting now."

I got up from my seat. "I'll go check in on him. I highly recommend the baked Mac and Cheese with garlic, Dusty." I let them talk and eat as I went to the infirmary.

The satyr was lying in a hospital bed. His left leg was in a white cast that ran all the way past his hip and was in a sling hung by a pulley system attached to the ceiling of the infirmary. A look of terror crossed his face the moment I entered the room. "Your Majesty, what you saw in Dusty's room was nothing!"

"You were holding Dusty's hand?" I asked. I sat down next to the bed in a swivel chair.

"Yes! Please don't have me executed!"

"I would never have you executed!"

"But Cassius said you knew about my private life, and Article 84 Section 17–."

"Is a horrible, barbaric law that I'm going to change when I get back to the castle. You shouldn't have to live in fear because you're gay, Gunther."

The satyr was taken back by my words. "You really mean it?"

"Of course, Eddie and I don't mind that you're gay. You're not just our employee, you're our friend. Eddie and I were very worried about you. I won't stand for bigotry and discrimination in

Peregrin which is why that law needs to change."

"The royals have never wanted to change it. I've lost so many friends over the years." Tears began to fill his eyes.

"Gunther, I'm so sorry for what my ancestors allowed. I can't change the past, but I can change the future. I've already written a new law that I would like you to look over when you're up to it."

"I don't know what to say, your Majesty." He reached over and grasped my hand in gratitude. He wiped away the tears with his free hand.

I smiled. Then I became serious. "Murad showed Eddie and I the video when you confronted him. You told him your friend died because of him. You were talking about your boyfriend, Enoch, weren't you?"

New tears began to form in the satyr's eyes as he let go of my hand. "Yes," he said softly.

"What happened?"

Gunther swallowed hard as he lay back on the pillow. "Three years ago, Enoch had a little bakery that had been passed down from his family for generations. Then Gordon

Bloodrayne came along and destroyed everything." His voice quavered as the tears began to flow down his cheeks. He bit his lower lip as he tried to regain his composure. "Bloodrayne was a part of the mob here, and Enoch was paying him for five hundred a month for 'protection' money. If Enoch couldn't pay, the shop would get vandalized or he would get beaten. He started losing business. One night, they beat Enoch so brutally that they nearly killed him. All because he had given Bloodrayne one of Murad's gems, and they found out it was fake. The next day, the bakery was burnt to the ground." He paused as he tried hard not to cry. "A week later, Enoch hung himself from a tree in our backyard." Gunther broke down and began to sob.

I said nothing, but let the satyr cry for a few minutes. I handed him the box of tissues by his bed. Finally, I spoke. "I am so sorry for your loss, Gunther."

The satyr nodded as he dabbed at the tears. "I miss him so much."

"How long were you and Enoch together?"

He smiled sadly. "10 years. "

"How did Enoch get a fake gem from Murad?"

Gunther sighed. "Accrding to his suicide note, Enoch had witnessed a kidnapping and was given the fake diamond with an anonymous note from the Mannequin King as payment for his silence or be killled. I began to look for the Mannequin King, but I had no leads to his whereabouts until a woman came by my home last week with information about Murad. She claimed to know where he was. I had to find him! I wanted him to pay for what happened to Enoch!"

I shook my head. I was angry at the portal devil. Murad's deceit had led to the faun's death and had left the satyr heartbroken. "Murad won't be ruining lives ever again," I told Gunther.

"What do you mean?"

"He's dead. My dad killed him in the arena."

"Good."

"What about the man Bloodrayne?"

Gunther shrugged. "I don't know. He disappeared after Enoch died." He looked at me, his eyes brimming with tears. "You're one of the few people who know about my relationship with Enoch. The royals have never been so kind to me."

"There are people here who know exactly what you're going through. Talk to my dad and stepmom because they can help you." I paused as I remembered someone who could help Gunther. "I would even talk to Dusty. He's been right in your shoes."

The satyr nodded. "I know. He told me he had lost his boyfriend, Chris, to suicide as well."

I nodded. "And if you can't find anyone to talk to, you can always talk to Eddie or myself." I got up from my seat and felt something in my pants pocket. "I almost forgot," I said as I reached in and pulled out the silver lighter. "I believe this belongs to you." I placed it in his hand.

Gunther gasped. "I thought I had lost this." He smiled through the tears. "Thank you so much, your Majesty."

I patted the satyr's shoulder. "I'll let you get some rest," I said. "I'm glad to have you back, Gunther."

When we arrived at Castle Delorean, I called all the members of my cabinet and asked them to attend an emergency meeting at the beginning of next week. A few things happened during those days. Dad accepted my offer to become the new royal cook. He and Amelia wanted to get out of the restaurant business for a few months.

Bruce, Libby, and their families went back to Zephyr, but Bruce and Libby were making arrangements to move to Peregrin after Dad suggested that Bruce become the assistant head cook. Andrew, Natalie, Jenny, Matt, and Dusty stayed in the castle as they wanted to rebuild their lives here in Peregrin.

The night before the meeting, Gunther joined Eddie and me in our suite after hours to read and go over the law. His leg had just gotten out of its cast thanks to the magic of the unicorn pills, but he still had to use a cane for a few weeks until his hip and leg were completely healed. He sat down at our kitchen table and graciously accepted the regular, black coffee we offered him.

Alonzo took this opportunity to jump on the table. The catnip dragon sniffed the satyr's coffee and recoiled back in disgust. In defiance, he turned around and lifted up his tail to Gunther.

"Alzono, get your butt out of Gunther's face!" I said to the catnip dragon as I scooped off of the table and set him down on the floor. He darted out of the kitchen, knocking the satyr's cane onto the kitchen floor in the process.

"Does your cane have a sword in it?" Eddie asked Gunther as he picked up the cane and leaned it against the table.

The satyr laughed. "Dusty asked me the same question on our date yesterday. He was disappointed to learn it's just an ordinary cane."

"Too bad," Eddie said.

Gunther smiled and then became serious. "I looked over the rewritten law, your Majesty," he said to me.

"What do you think?" I asked.

"Aside from a few grammatical errors, it's wonderful." He sighed. "I really want this new law to happen. For once in my life, I would like to be able to hold hands or kiss in public without having to look over my shoulder constantly. Especially with Dusty."

"You really like him, don't you?" Eddie asked.

Gunther nodded "We've already started seeing each other, in secret of course. I had to do the same with Enoch, and I'm tired of living in fear for my life." He swallowed hard. He was silent for a moment. "To get a law passed here in Peregrin, there are two steps you must take, your Majesties."

I nodded. "Other than talking with the cabinet members, what's the next step?"

"If the cabinet approves, then you must go before parliament to have them approve it."

"How long will that take?" Eddie asked.

"Up to a day at the most."

"Wow! Government moving fast, that's a first," I said.

"That's only if the cabinet will approve of the Equality Act," Gunther said as a worried look came across his face.

"Gunther, you've gotta have faith. I'm sure it will get passed."

"What if it doesn't?"

"Then Shelly and I will keep pushing until it does. We Van Helsings don't give up that easily," Eddie assured him.

"Gunther," I said, "I don't want you coming to the cabinet

meeting tomorrow."

The satyr knew why. "If I'm there, I might kill Dr. Orlock if he disagrees."

"The last thing I want is to get the carpet in the conference room dry cleaned," I joked.

"I'll call in sick," Gunther said. "Shall we get to work?"

To say, I was nervous the next morning was an understatement. I barely ate my breakfast of scrambled eggs and toast for fear of it coming back up. I grabbed the multiple copies of the newly edited law before Eddie and I headed downstairs to the closed conference room doors. I took a deep breath of courage before opening them up.

We weren't as early as we thought we were. Around the conference table was every single member of my cabinet all looking at me with uncertainty. I took a seat at the head of the table with Eddie by my side and placed the copies face down in front of me. "Have a seat, everyone," I said as I gestured around the room at the six members.

"Where is Mr. Hornicus?" Doctor Orlock asked. He had

immediately noticed my private secretary's absence.

"He's out sick today," I explained. "The king has offered to take notes in his absence." There was a short pause before I continued. "It has come to my attention that there is a law in Peregrin that must be abolished right away."

Everyone began murmuring as they tried to figure out which law I was referring to. My minister of finance, a werewolf banker named Reggie Loup, thought it could be about changing the exchange rate while the minister of commerce, a lovely centaur named Christabelle Shadowfax, thought I wanted to close down the newly opened trade routes. Only Cassius, my minister of transportation, remained silent.

"Article 84 Section 17.1." My words stopped the conversations abruptly and hung in the air like a storm cloud ready to explode. "The law is barbaric, and I will not tolerate bigotry and discrimination in my queendom." I went around the table and handed each member a copy of the Equality Act. "This new law will replace Article 84 Section 17.1." *Because*, I thought to myself, *apparently you need to have laws to tell people not to be jerks to each other.* I waited patiently for them to look it over and comment.

I didn't have to wait long. Less than thirty seconds in, Doctor Orlock, the Minister of Virtue exploded. "This is unacceptable! If this law replaces Article 84 Section 17.1, you know what will happen, your Majesty!"

Bigots like yourself will be exposed, I thought. Instead, I said, " The members of the LBGT+ community will not live in fear?"

"The morals of the queendom will go downhill. Marriage between these abominations? Allowing them to adopt children just to ruin the children's lives?"

At least, Orlock wasn't making some ridiculous argument about underage marriage. I was already at my boiling point. "Just how would a gay or lesbian couple ruin children's lives?" I asked, keeping my temper under control.

"By abusing them, of course!"

"So, straight couples have never abused their children?" General Nessa Wulfsguard, my minister of defense asked..

Way to go, General, I thought.

The vampire wheeled on the werewolf. "Are you one of

them?"

"No, but I'm not a bigot."

"Neither am I," the werelion minister of state, Hamish Lionheart, replied. He looked at me. "I agree with your decision, your Majesty. Article 84 Section 17.1 has gone on for much too long." The other cabinet members nodded in agreement.

"This is madness!" shouted Orlock. "These people are an abomination!"

I had enough of Doctor Orlock's bigotry. "No one should have to live in fear because of who they love, Doctor Orlock."

I barely registered Eddie's chair scraping back against the floor. He quickly stood up and placed his hands on the table as he leaned against it. "I grew up in a town where vampires were discriminated against," my husband said. "We were shunned and killed. When I became one, I was disowned by my own family and forced to live on the streets all because of who I was. I hate people who discriminate against others. I stand with the queen, my wife, against bigotry and discrimination against the LBGT+ community." Eddie sat back down.

Everyone was quiet, even Doctor Orlock, for once. Finally,

the Prime Minister, a celestial being, spoke. "I agree with the king and queen. I vote yes on passing the Equality Act." This was a huge deal to have the pamola agree with the queen and the king as Eddie and I could not vote on this matter. "If it's alright with your Majesty," Hiram looked at me. I gave my nod of approval."let's place our votes on the matter. All in favor of abolishing Article 84 Section 17.1 and instating the new Equality Act, raise your hand."

My heart thudded against my chest as they began to vote. I felt my husband reach under the table and squeeze my hand reassuringly. I didn't realize I had been holding my breath as I watched ten hands go up.

"All against?" Hiram asked.

The only hand that went up belonged to the Minister of Virtue. Shocking, I know. "This is a big mistake, your Majesty." His seething words filled with venom." You are bringing immorality into our great queendom."

Hiram blatantly ignored Doctor Orlock and continued. "So be it. Let the record stand. On this day and at this time, the cabinet of Queen Michelle has voted 11-1 to allow the Equality

Act to go before Parliament."

Doctor Orlock immediately stormed out of the conference room, slamming the door behind him. *Too bad the door didn't hit you in the rear on the way out,* I thought. I focused back on the other cabinet members. "Does anyone else have any other items they wish to bring to the meeting?"

Once the meeting concluded an hour later, Eddie and I went back into my office to call Gunther with the news. I made sure to shut the door to keep the phone conversation private. "I've got good news," I told the satyr once he answered. "The cabinet voted 11-1 in favor of the Equality Act!"

He was speechless for a moment. Finally, he spoke, and I could hear the hope in his voice, "I can't believe this is actually happening!"

"Believe it."

"Was Doctor Orlock the one who voted against it?"

"Let's just say everyone knows how much of a bigot the guy really is."

"Wow!"

"Yep! He showed his true colors and then some."

Gunther sighed. "Can't say I'm surprised. When are you going to Parliament?"

"Tomorrow afternoon. Gunther, if you'd like, you and Dusty are more than welcome to stay here at the castle until the Equality Act is passed." I was concerned for their safety, especially after Orlock's unruly display at the meeting.

"I'd appreciate that, your Majesty."

Chapter Thirteen:

Life-Changing News and an Odd Thank You

The next day was very busy and tense for me. I spent half of the morning writing and rewriting my speech to Parliament. Then I spent the afternoon pleading my case to the representatives of the various inhabited islands. My nerves were so shot that I don't remember what my speech was about, but Eddie told me later it was powerful and thought-provoking. The head of the house thanked me for my time and told me they would vote on the act by the end of the night.

Around six that evening, Eddie and I were making supper when we heard knocking on the door to our suite. Alonzo perked up at the sound and readied himself to dart his way to freedom. I set the last fork on the table and scooped the catnip dragon before I opened the door. "Come in, guys," I told Gunther and Dusty.

The two men walked in, and Alonzo squirmed out of my arms. Dusty immediately closed the door before the little dragon could make a break for it. "Hey, there, little guy," Dusty said as he squatted down and scratched Alonzo between the ears. "What's your name?"

"Alonzo," I said.

The catnip dragon sniffed Dusty's hand a few more times before deciding he was allowed to enter into his domain. Then Alonzo randomly ran back to hide in our bedroom.

I eyed the box under Dusty's free arm. "Can I take that for you?"

"Oh, sure," he said. "Gunther and I weren't sure if you and Eddie drank so we brought dessert instead."

I lifted up the round box's cover and smiled. "Hey, Eddie, Gunther and Dusty brought a strawberry cheesecake!" I shouted to my husband who was still in the kitchen.

"Excellent!"

Gunther smiled. "Thank you for inviting us over to wait for the results from parliament, your Majesty." He leaned heavily on his cane as he looked for a place to sit down.

I motioned for him to sit down at the kitchen table. "You know you can call me Shelly," I told him.

"But that would be disrespectful, your Majesty," Gunther said as he limped over. He went to grab a chair, but Dusty got there first. The satyr smiled as he watched the former police detective pull it out for him.

"Okay," I said as I finished setting the silverware next to the plates. I understood that he wanted to be formal with me and Eddie, but I also wanted him to feel comfortable. "How about this compromise? At work, you can address me and Eddie formally. After work, you can be casual. Will that work for you?"

He thought about it for a few moments and then smiled. "It will."

Eddie came out of the kitchen with a steaming hot pan of garlic eggplant lasagna. He set it down on the kitchen table. "I hope you're hungry."

"Of course," I said as we all sat down, "I'm starving!"

Alonzo came out of hiding and curled up next to my chair. Once Eddie cut each of us a piece off his creation, I bit into it. "Nothing like a home-cooked meal."

Dusty had taken a seat next to Gunther and took a bite. "Is this eggplant?"

Eddie nodded. "Yep. This is one of Shelly's favorite dishes."

"You did a great job, Shelly," Dusty said. "This is delicious!"

I pointed to my husband with my fork. "Eddie's the chef." "Could I have this recipe?" Dusty asked.

"Yeah, I found it online when Shelly and I were dating."

I looked at the vampire. "You told me it was an old family recipe."

Eddie lifted up a finger. "I was right, it's somebody's old family recipe."

I playfully punched him in the arm as I chuckled. "You're a dork," I said.

"That's why you love me, right?" Eddie said with a grin.

Our guests smiled at us. Then Dusty slipped an arm

around Gunther, and Eddie and I noticed how comfortable the satyr was with the intimate touch from the man. "This is a vegetarian meal," Dusty said. "You guys are vampires. I thought you just drank blood."

"No, we can eat regular food," I explained. "I drink fruit dragon blood, but it's more like a dietary supplement. Vampires don't have to rely on it. Blood does help us heal faster, but that's about it."

"Except I can't drink blood," Eddie said.

"Moral reasons?" Gunther asked.

"No, a rare blood allergy. I get violently sick if I digest blood," Eddie explained.

"I didn't realize that, sire-I mean, Eddie," Gunther replied.

"No problem," Eddie said.

"Shelly, did you become a vampire when you came to this world?" Dusty asked.

"No," I said as I absentmindedly reached for my neck. "I've only been a vampire for a few I months."

"You were turned?" Dusty asked.

"Unwillingly," I said.

Eddie knew how uncomfortable I was and put an arm around me. "The last queen sent a vampire assassin after Shelly, and he was the one who turned her."

Dusty seemed to understand I had no desire to talk about it anymore.

The rest of the dinner went very smoothly. Gunther was visibly nervous as we still hadn't heard the results. Instead, we talked about other things to get his mind off Parliament. We talked about Dusty's future here in Peregrin. He was considering getting a job as a charter fisherman but did offer his assistance as security here at the castle. He discovered his magical ability when he accidentally opened up a hole in the ground on the way to Gunther's house. After much discussion, Eddie informed Dusty that he had the ability to manipulate the earth. Gunther also accepted my idea of getting him an assistant. I told him he could sit in on the interviews if he wished.

As I was about to clear off the table and retrieve the strawberry cheesecake, three loud knocks on the suite's door made us all jump. I looked at Eddie in confusion. "Is anyone else coming over?"

My husband shook his head, and I went to the door to investigate. I unlocked it and was about to turn the handle when Eddie was by my side, war scythe in hand. He stood to the side and gave me the go-ahead to open it up. I slowly creaked the door open and saw no one in the hallway. Something white on the floor caught my eye. I looked down at the envelope and almost picked it up. It was addressed to me and my husband in perfect block letters. "Gunther, did you or Dusty drop an envelope when you came in?"

"No, we didn't." Gunther grabbed his cane, and he and Dusty joined us at the front door. He inspected the envelope without touching it. "I don't recognize the handwriting."

"Neither do I," I said.

Eddie kept looking up and down the empty hallway. He bent down, retrieved a small handgun from an ankle holster, and gave it to Dusty. "Get back inside with Gunther and lock the door, Shelly."

Alonzo poked his little head between our legs to ponder if he could escape down the hall. "That means you too, Alonzo," Eddie told the catnip dragon as he quickly scooped him up in his arms and handed him over to me. Alonzo looked at us with innocence in his green eyes.

"Dusty, do you mind helping me search the floor?" Eddie asked.

"Not at all," Dusty said, and he and my husband started their sweep of the floor.

I shut and locked the door. As I set Alonzo on the floor, I noticed the worried look on the satyr's face. "I don't think this has anything to do with the Equality Act."

"Okay," Gunther said, but his tone indicated he was not fully convinced. He limped back to the kitchen table and sat down. "The staff has gone home for the evening, correct?" I nodded. Only my staff and my family knew the access elevator code to get to our suite. I began to wonder if it was the mystery woman. "We've been having some security issues."

The satyr raised an eyebrow. "What do you mean?" As I told him about Colleen, his eyes widened in shock. "That can't be right! The Colleen I met was a fairy!"

"You mean this person impersonated an architect?"

"No." He shook his head vigorously. "The day before I

took off, a fairy named Colleen came to my house. She told me she was a former customer of Enoch's. She gave me the coordinates to Murad's hotel." Gunther paused. "I don't know how she knew about the gem because it was never published in any of the news outlets." He shook his head. "I should've asked her more questions, but I had been crying all day and wasn't thinking straight."

"Don't worry about it, Gunther. I get it. Around the anniversary of my mom's death, I'm not my normal self." I poured myself and the satyr a glass of water.

I heard someone knocking the first few notes of Queen's "We Will Rock You." on the front door. I got up from the table. "Eddie and Dusty are back."

I opened the door and let the men inside. "Find anything?" I asked.

Eddie shook his head as he pressed the button on Vengeance. The blade on the top of the war scythe slid into the staff before the whole thing collapsed down to a short stick. "No one was on our floor, but we think they took the elevator. How they knew the code is beyond me." He handed me the envelope.

"It's safe. I can't detect any powders or devices."

I slowly opened it up and pulled out a neatly folded piece of ordinary copy paper. "All it says is 'Thank you. It's signed by Colleen."

"For what?" Eddie asked.

"Who's Colleen?" Dusty asked. "The only person I know by that name was a woman who came to the police station to inform Andrew and me about Matt's whereabouts."

Eddie and I looked at each other. "Did she have black sparkly hair?" I asked.

"Yes, how did you know?" I quickly told him about the mystery woman. "So, who is she really? And why is she thanking you?" The police detective asked.

"Don't know," I said as we all sat back down again. An idea popped into my head. I quickly got up. "Be right back." I ran into my bedroom and looked around for a pen and a piece of paper. Once I had found them in one of our dresser drawers, I brought the items back to the kitchen table. "Okay, let's do a timeline of this mystery woman," I said as I turned the paper horizontally and drew a straight line across the middle of the page. "First encounter with her. She was human." I drew a small tick near the start of the line and wrote human next to it.

"Right," Dusty said. He craned his neck to get a better look at the timeline

"Then she approached me as a fairy," Gunther said.

I made another tick and wrote fairy.

"She came to you and me as a minotaur," Eddie added.

"Then she posed as a Winged One to Marcie," I said as I added another mark to the timeline. "Anyone else she has posed as?" I asked.

They all shook their heads. "She might be a shapeshifter," Dusty suggested. He glanced at Gunther. "You guys have them here, right?"

Gunther nodded. "Some people do, but they usually can only shapeshift into one specific thing."

"And," Eddie added. "They normally show up on camera."

Gunther looked surprised. "What do you mean?"

Eddie quickly explained Robin's phone interaction with the mysterious Colleen. "I had Archer go back over the footage once we realized she was a fraud. There was no sign of her showing up anywhere on the security cameras."

Gunther glanced at Dusty who was furrowing his brow in thought. "What's wrong?" he asked.

"I just realized something. When the woman Colleen first came to the police, she asked for Timothy, specifically."

I was taken aback. "I don't understand. Why was she asking for my dad?"

Dusty shrugged. "I don't know. When we told her your family had died in that house fire, she just said Matt was still alive and being forced to mine fake gems. Then she left the station, and we never heard from her again."

I shook my head and was about to ask for more details when a thought struck me. "How did she get from world to world?"

"Maybe she's a portal devil," Dusty suggested.

Something in my gut told me that wasn't right, but I knew I couldn't say anything. I had no tangible evidence to say either way. My cell phone vibrating in my pants pockets distracting everyone. I pulled out and glanced at the caller ID."It's Hiram." I saw Gunther look over at the man he was dating and gripped his hand. I picked up the phone and went into the kitchen for privacy.

"Hello!" I said after answering it.

"Your Majesty, this is Hiram."

"Hello, Hiram," I said, trying to calm my nerves.

"Parliament has voted on your law."

I glanced at the kitchen table. Gunther and Dusty were still holding hands and nervously looking at each other. They needed this. Everyone needed this. I swallowed hard. "And?"

"583 to 40 in favor of abolishing Article 84 Section 17.1 and replacing it with the Equality Act."

I don't know how I did it, but I managed to contain my excitement. I maintained a straight face as I thanked the prime minister for calling me with the news. Once he hung up, I grabbed the cheesecake out of the fridge and brought it to the table. "It passed!" I nearly shouted with a big smile. I set the dessert on the table before I dropped it with my excitement.

The worry vanished from the satyr's face and was replaced with happiness. He let go of Dusty's hand and embraced him. Then the two men kissed as tears of joy filled their eyes.

Eddie quietly got up and stood beside me. He put his arm around me and whispered, "You did good." He kissed me.

Gunther pulled away from Dusty and stood up with the aid of his cane. He walked over and gave me and Eddie a big hug. "Thank you so much for all you've done, both of you," he said as he wiped away his tears.

"You're welcome, Gunther," I said, returning the hug.

"Gunther was right about you, Shelly," Dusty replied as he got up from the table. He gave both Eddie and I a hug. "You're a great queen."

I blushed. "Thanks," I said. "I just wanted to right my ancestors' wrongs."

Gunther wobbled as he stood. Dusty reached out to support him and helped him back to his chair. He gave a grateful nod. "I'm still not used to these pins in my hip." Once we were all sitting back down, he raised his glass. "May I propose a toast?"

"Of course," I said as I quickly filled up everyone else's glasses with water. "Go on, Gunther."

"To Queen Shelly for overturning a hateful law to make a better queendom for Dusty, myself and the rest of the gay community."

"To Queen Shelly!" Eddie and Dusty echoed as they raised their glasses.

I raised my glass. "To Gunther and Dusty, may you find happiness and freedom from now on."

"Here, here!"

I began to cut out a piece of the delicious dessert. "How about a piece of this celebratory cheesecake?"

COMING SOON

Presents of the Undead

My Life Among the Undead:

Book 11

By
Camara M. Bragdon

In the land of Peregrin, the newly crowned queen and king, Shelly and Eddie Van Helsing, are in for an adventurous Christmas. Shelly is astonished to discover that Santa Claus is real and residing in Ho Hoboken, where the holiday spirit is waning. A conflict between the elves and sasquatch security has halted the toy shop's production, with Mrs. Claus missing. To complicate matters, Santa is unfazed by the chaos. Shelly and Eddie must brave the icy wilderness to save the day. However, there's more to Santa than meets the eye, and Mrs. Claus's vanishing act is just the beginning. As they journey through the frosty terrain, they will uncover the startling truth about the merry man in red.

ABOUT THE AUTHOR

Camara M. Bragdon lives in sunny southwest Florida with her cat. Mistoffelees. When she is not writing, she brings joy and learning as a children's and teen librarian, taking pictures and telling terrible puns.This is the tenth book in her vampire series, *My Life among the Undead*. Visit her website at www.camarambragdonauthor.com